Disclaimer: The Publisher and the Author make no representation or warranties concerning the accuracy or completeness of the contents of this work and specifically disclaim all warranties for a particular purpose. No warranty may be created or extended through sales or promotional materials. The advice and strategies contained herein may not be suitable for every situation. This work is sold with the understanding that the Author and Publisher are not engaged in rendering legal, technological, or other professional services. If professional assistance is required, the services of a competent professional should be sought. Neither the Publisher nor the Author shall be liable for damages arising therefrom.

The fact that an organization or website is referred to in this work as a citation and/or potential source of further information does not mean that the Author or the Publisher endorses the information, the organization, or website it may provide, or recommendations it may make. Further, readers should be aware that websites listed in this work may have changed or disappeared between when this work was written and when it is read. Disclaimer: The cases and stories in this book have had details changed to preserve privacy.

Paperback ISBN: ISBN: 978-1-64873-391-8
EBOOK ISBN: 978-1-64873-392-5

Printed in the United States of America
Published by:
Writer's Publishing House
Prescott, AZ 86301

Cover Design: Creative Artistic Excellence

The Bison

By Karen J. Keim

Bison and calf, c. 1866, South Dakota

1890 Great South Western Plains

The baked earth lay pummeled behind the lead beast who broke through the sunlit air with a weight of just over one ton. Four angry hooves beat at the ground in an effort to gain momentum and space between the herd and the iron machine pumping along its track, paralleling their path. Steam billowed from the engineś black funnel-shaped smoke stack as the twelve-car train reached speeds far able to out-distance a horse of good breeding, much more so the densely muscled and boned buffalo in any race. A crack sounded from a window of the train, and then another, and one of the herd fell, its hips rolling over its head, and small clouds of dirt floating upwards over the body as it settled to a still mound of rust-colored hide, expelling one final breath.

The lead beastś small wild eyes turned back to view the fall, and pulled forward to move the rest of the herd onward. The year was 1890.

One passenger sitting in the third railroad car was a girl, alone, except for a white dog laying at her side on the brown-upholstered bench next to her. She blinked awake in the light coming through the dusty window glass. Her long hair of gold-blasted copper was braided over a shoulder, and she stretched, glancing at Toby who lay curled up unmoving, long nose pressed against her leg. The rifle explosions apparently had awakened the traveler from a dreamless nap. As she felt the train moving beneath her, the loud clack-clack of the iron wheels rolling over the track brought her back into the early morning. Tabitha Martin was sixteen years old, and her life as she'd known it was forever changed. She was careening towards an unknown destination, disappearing into what she knew only as the "Wild, Wild West," according to reports in the New York Times. Her tall, blonde-haired, beautiful mother had put her on this train. Two leather trunks held all of her belongings, and she would meet a father she'd never seen before; she never felt so alone, nor so alive.

Transcontinental Railway c. 1879

Historically, this tragedy happened according to reporting publications as often as the transcontinental railroad had made its way across the vast plains connecting from the east coast to the west of America. At the time, it was looked upon as a consequence of travelers' boredom, one of a few ways for passengers to pass the long hours of travel time. No one then saw it as cruel, hurtful, or as a punitive action. Thoughts of contributing to the species' endangerment or extinction was never of any concern in these times.

There were millions of buffalo, whose prime purpose was providing necessary food and clothing, by grazing, living and procreating on the great plains, for the tribes of the first natives of America. At the hand of the White Man, they were fast becoming merely targets for practice by anyone with a firearm. In all the years of this killing sport, not one soul spoke up in defense of this atrocity, which was causing innumerable quantities of the species to disappear. Certainly, no thought of the action as damaging the food supply of the many plains Indians was ever wasted.

One fact was interesting; no woman was ever documented in having fired a single shot.

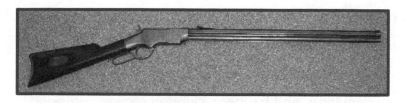

Winchester Long Gun

Luke cinched the saddle strap to the third hole position around the belly of Charlotte, his Appaloosa, and placed his foot into the stirrup to swing himself up into the saddle. As sheriff of the town of Prescott during the impending statehood of Arizona, he had enjoyed his job that started at the crack of dawn every day but Sunday. He held his office over two deputies, and they were the overseers of the whole of Yavapai County.

It was a beautiful April morning. He could just make out the San Francisco Peaks in the distant north, still covered with snow from a cold, late winter storm. He didn't know it yet, but within ten years, this area of Flagstaff would be known as the Snow Bowl skiing mecca that would attract skiers from all over the country, as well as the site of the Lowell Observatory, which would help NASA to navigate Apollo 13 to the moon as a result of its 7,000 foot altitude.

But in 1890, it was just a beautiful site to see in the far distance.

Luke's tan ten-gallon hat shaded his eyes from the bright sunshine, and his deer-skinned gloves tightened around the reins to direct the mare east along the dirt road that ran in front of his small ranch. Today he was taking the long two-day trip to Fort Yuma to meet a train that would arrive in two days. He would stop on his way to a neighboring ranch first because he needed to pick up a light buckboard so he could bring his daughter to his Prescott home. He had no idea if she knew how to ride horseback. He'd never met her. He'd been unaware of her existence until two months ago, after he'd received a letter arriving in his post office box from Philadelphia, Pennsylvania from his ex-wife, Sophia, who had left him one day without a word.

She was apparently sending their daughter to him. The letter had been short, curt and contained no explanation. She had simply asked Luke to take good care of her, and signed off as Mrs. S. Martin. Apparently, she'd been remarried since their parting.

Sheriff Richmond, with all he'd seen and experienced in his 35 years on earth was full of trepidation in his gut; he'd never been so spooked, so unprepared, so anxious.

He'd been Sheriff of the mountainous town and adjacent valley, soon to be named Lonesome Valley (today Prescott Valley) and had managed peace within the law of this area, once part of the New Mexico Territory, after the American-Mexican War earlier in the decade. This was the real Wild West; men were gun-toting and women needed to be willing and able to pull their weight in a time and place scarce in fineries, luxuries and ease. The settlers had crossed the prairies of the Midwest in covered wagons pulled by horses and mules; some came only atop mules or on foot. Arizona was home to the Apache and the Navajo communities, along with various smaller tribes. Their peace came in between periodic conflicts. Luke had been in dangerous situations during his time working side-by-side with the prior sheriff, then after his passing, on his own. Soon, there were less tribal fights compared to Native-White Man attacks.

Today he was imagining himself relating to a sixteen-year-old girl who belonged to him. His daughter. His blood. He'd thought about Sophie often, obviously at first when he realized she had left him. He'd only guessed that she'd returned to her parents back east, to New York City. As time pressed on, she became a faded memory and he'd accepted her absence, storing every piece of her into one upstairs bedroom behind a closed door. He'd been with very few other women since his wife left, apparently after discovering that she was pregnant.

As he came upon his neighbor Cliff's land, Charlotte neighed, knowing her way to this ranch. She turned automatically in through the open wooden gate. Luke's whole life was about to change.

Charlotte

For Tabitha, there was thankfully a break in travel as passengers were allowed to disembark from their train cars for a full hour to stretch their legs, and visit the Union Station in St. Louis, Missouri. There was a Mercantile to eat at and shop for needs, and the use of an outhouse after their long, long trek on the the brand new Santa Fe Passenger Train. This was a new way to travel, in that it was combined with cargo cars, trailing seated travelers with supplies from eastern cities to stock western stores, shops, and privately ordered goods.

The Transcontinental Railroad Project connecting America's east to its west was a miracle of the day; a magnificent merging of a highly increasing economic boom in a country whose entire expanse was still not 100% known. It was the nearing of the end of 19th century life and the major part of the growth in the country, turning territories into states, adding to the United States of America's population, expansion and progress. It was an exciting time.

It was also a time of tension. Arizona and New Mexico made a home to several settlers' families as well as Native American tribes and the Mexican population from the south. It was the post-Civil War era and the country was scrambling in the southeast to undergo reconstruction; others went west in a hurry to settle homesteads. The work to incorporate towns and establish relevant and profitable businesses, which started with residents of the White population in a still-foreign country was bound to cause friction. It was the time of opportunity to find and use undiscovered natural resources. But the traditional culture of a population of natives who'd been living in the deserts and on the plains of this vast country were in place, having adapted to the harshness of the land, and were much more experienced in navigating into inhabiting the environment successfully.

The reality was that the Wild West was quickly becoming the White Man's world. Women were second class citizens...the followers...the obedient wives of strong young men who'd adventured into the future. They were meant to keep home fires burning, food prepared, and rear the children. They were to dress conservatively, say little, work hard, and bear many sons to populate and spread the White race throughout the virgin land to eventually take over this land.

It was also a great time of freedom, and sometimes that led to a surge of anarchy of a kind . . . lawlessness, crime, theft... 19th century gang mindsets. Laws differed from area to area, even within a state or a territory. Sheriffs were simply brave or imbecilic men who wanted to do something different, something significant, but often were just "figureheads" that wore a uniform, a tin badge, toted a gun and spent time, usually alone or with an inexperienced deputy trying to map out their very jobs. Their workplace was usually in a plain, dusty, windowless room on a muddy Main Street. They were provided with a horse, a saddle and a firearm. Lockup could be a cell, or just an area in back until the trial or decision to let them go free or be transferred to a larger community where the security was more sophisticated. The wild west societal geography was being crafted day by day. It made for an exciting yet unpredictable era.

This was the world Tabitha was about to enter. Even though she moved quietly and unobtrusively among the other passengers, she didn't shrink from holding her head high, stepping lightly, never going anywhere without her Bull Terrier, Toby. He was English bred and was completely devoted to his mistress. He paralleled her left leg with every step she took. He was stark white. He was muscled, alert and protective. He was a gift from her mother, who loved everything British. Breathing in the dry air, crunching soil beneath her kid-leathered boots, and holding her parasol overhead, she felt a strange sense of vastness, freedom and a new beginning. It made her smile. It attracted anyone near her to her statuesque, graceful beauty; however, the stiffness and pomp she came away from somehow was shedding itself from within her with each gust of the warm gales traveling across these prairies surrounding her.

Toby

Sophia Mary York found herself unable to tolerate the married life she'd found herself in sixteen years earlier. She had found the Wild West much too raw and barren for her taste. When she found out that she was pregnant with Tabitha, she decided to flee home to Philadelphia, to her parent's mansion in Parkway Heights. She'd raised her daughter there for two years under her parent's roof, until she met Mr. Randolph Martin, of First National Bank, which had several operations in the states starting early in the 19th century by a cousin of his: John Pierpont Morgan. A wealthy bachelor of fifty years in age, he'd met the beautiful and intelligent woman at a soiree of the governor's, staying close to her mother and father as they mingled among other rich elites in the grand ballroom of New York's Plaza Hotel. After gazing at her until it would be considered rude ogling, he'd asked around to find that this lovely vision was in fact a single mother living at her parent's mansion in Philadelphia. He asked her parents for her hand, as they were of the same cloth, and after a very public and elaborate wedding, he whisked her away to his life in New York.

Randolph agreed to formally adopt her daughter, and since Sophia was well-used to a privileged style that suited her just fine.

Mrs. Sophia Boudreau Richmond Martin, c. 1870

Approximately thirty-six Native American tribes lived in North America, existing long before 1492; at one time, an approximation of 18 million souls were settled here prior to European immigration.

Their interaction with Pilgrims c. 1600 was with mostly Choctaw tribe members. They had, at first, an amiable relationship. The indigenous men and women welcomed the pale, tall strangers into their lives and taught them where to hunt, fish, and how to plant crops and acclimate themselves to the different weather and climate they were completely unprepared for. They had lived in towns within houses with a much more sophisticated way of doing the simplest of tasks. Yet, because of their sense of community, perhaps their religious practices and desire to start a new life different from what they had left behind, they were willing to be taught. They were also able to impart intelligence in a practical way to the native men and women. It was a time of sharing and joining in abilities to not only survive but to flourish.

Their gifts to the natives were to teach them their language and religion, share some of their possessions that were foreign to them and of course, and miracles according to their understanding. Muskets, fitted cloth clothing, pots and pans, utensils, and other items from their culture were unknown. How many Native American young ladies had seen a petticoat, a bustle, a corset, a feathered hat? Where would they have come into contact with cobbled shoes, lace, silk? They were living the epitome of "life au naturel" from head to toe, from cooking and hunting, to living quarters and use of resources they were privy to.

And so, it comes full circle back to this: after the mighty Bison had been shot from a train, and lay under the hot, Midwest sun for a week, what was left for them to use?

The horns for weapons for protection and hunting, and if the hide hadn't decomposed yet from maggots that were spread inside the meat and edible organs, they might be able to use some of the hide for shelter and warmth. But, perhaps some may say the greatest waste to these indigenous people was wasting the beautiful beast that had so many uses for their very survival, thus, the reason for slaughter of the Bison.

Yavapai Family, North Central Arizona, c. 1850

Yuma Town was only about five miles from what is today the boundary of Mexico on the US southern border...small and dusty, a small community beside the Colorado River. Luke had traveled through these mountains, heavily populated with tall Ponderosa pines, stark, open desert, Yucca Tree and Saguaro cacti, and a stream or two. He carried water in the wagon behind him. The team of Draft horses he'd traded Charlotte for clip-clopped side-by-side smoothly and were a well-matched team. Luke had slept in the wagon on his bed roll near Vicksburg overnight. He was hot, tired, sweaty and hungry when he came up on the town's main street.

His pocket watch read he was two hours early before the train was due. He checked into the livery stable to have the stable hand water, feed and brush down the horses, and then paid for a half-day small room with a shower. He watched the dirt disappear into the drain as the water poured over him. He was only used to a bath to clean himself in so this was new to him but he made a note to himself to construct one in his house.

He used the one towel to dry off and changed into his good white shirt. He cleaned up his hat as best he could, and shined up his boots. Belt and holster strapped on, he chose not to shave, and he was ready to go.

He studied his reflection for a moment in the wall mirror. His hair was reddish brown, and he sported a mustache and now faint beard. His blue eyes were clear and bright and his skin well- tanned. A square jawed smirk under a well-shaped nose stared back at him. He was in very fit shape as he worked almost daily and part of those days were atop a horse or working his ranch. He pulled on his saddlebag over his shoulder and left the room.

He stopped for a beer at the saloon downstairs. The roman numeral clock above the mirrored backdrop of the long polished bar showed he still had one-half of an hour before her train would pull into the station, and he would certainly hear the steel giant approach and whistle when the Santa Fe train arrived. As he sipped at his glass of tapped beer, he slowly considered meeting this stranger, his daughter.

What would she look like? Would she resemble him at all, or look more like her mother? Would she have a million questions? Would she be silent and angry? Would she even want to be here? He knew nothing about her except for her existence. His ex-wife, whom he'd never formally divorced, had certainly been a beauty. He'd watched as she struggled to fit into an Arizona life, but obviously was not able to tolerate it.

Sophia . . .. he closed his eyes and her image floated into his head, and even a mite into his heart.

They'd met in such a haphazard way, with there being no reason for them to believe that their pairing was meant to be, but, even though he'd gone for years not knowing the reason why they had married just to have her leave him in less than a year, now he finally realized…was Tabitha that reason?

Suddenly, calamitously, the great Santa Fe Railroad engine blew once, twice. Luke left his beer half-full. He was going to meet his daughter and he set out for the station on foot.

Yuma RR Station Saloon

Downtown Prescott Town and Lonesome Valley were a dual community. Prescott had two saloons, a Mercantile, Livery Stable, three hotels, two restaurants, and one Grain and Feed store. There were two churches established in clapboard buildings, one Baptist, one Mormon. The town schoolhouse held classes in one of the two Baptist Church buildings. The classroom was the adjacent building to the sanctuary and had two long tables with benches. There was a counter and a sink with cupboards for storage of foodstuffs. A wood-burning pot-bellied stove sat in a corner of the room mainly for heating the large room, but also able to heat water on the iron top.

The valley had huge grain and feed stores, stockyards filled with cattle and horses for auction and sale of livestock, and spread-out ranches and farm land with less populated dwellings. This was high desert land, one mile high. In winter the snow covered the ground; in summer, the sun scalded that same high desert soil, and the residents thanked God for the towering shade trees of Cottonwood and Blue Spruce dotted all throughout the area.

There were Caucasian, Mexican and Natives of many tribes living here. There was a Chinese influx, due only to the laying of rails for the train track to join east and west. There was also an influx of diverse immigrants because of the mining industry. Arizona was well known for silver and copper mining, and somewhat substantially in the southeast, gold was found. It was never considered a valuable resource to the native tribes, but the Whites saw opportunity with news of veins of ore discovered. There were three silver mines, three copper mines and one gold mine well-established since the early 1800's.

Arizona had few schools. Renee Boudreau was the teacher at the school here in Prescott. Her parents were part of the Mid-Century Southern Movement that chose to explore and expand the great western settlement from

Louisiana. They had never believed nor wanted to tolerate slavery in their lives, and so were compelled to settle in a place where such human indignities did not exist. Her father was a Baptist preacher.

They had passed away during an Apache raid north of Flagstaff. She and her older brother had survived, and lived together in their modest cabin, fortunately not burned down. They'd seen their parents, as little children, die in a skirmish in the Maricopa area between Apache warriors and Whites during the increasing tension between White and Indian fighting that consistently broke out.

Renee's parents had migrated here from France in search of a new life, and were hopeful about a better future for their children. They were loving, and hard working. She still missed them today. She and her brother moved in with another family and when Paul was eighteen, the two moved south to Prescott to leave the tragic past behind and begin again with the same hope their parents had.

Paul secured a job as a hand with a rancher of Texas Longhorn cattle, who let them both live on the property in a small abode. Renee was an avid learner and took a certificated course when she reached eighteen so that she could teach children in need of an education.

She was now 25 years old, and content with her job, her cat, her house and her brother's support and company. Neither of them had married. But of course, and probably for them both, there was something missing besides the part of their hearts that remembered their brutally-killed parents. They needed to find an outside love to fill them with joy. Joy was not currently a part of their lives. They had come to accept this as their way of life. But of course, laying still in the dark underneath her quilt, Renee fantasized about having a family of her own.

Renee was the one and only teacher at the school, working with students from age six up to sixteen. Two mothers volunteered at various times to assist her. They used the books available to them and the sparse materials, such as paper, pencils, chalk and boards for educating the growing population in Mathematics, English reading and writing skills and History.

Renee shared her personal library accrued over the years by her parents and thus her, and begged, borrowed and purchased books to build a small starting library, as well as any materials that would aid her in her teaching. She loved working with students, young and old. She would come in early, lighting the kerosene lanterns and stoking the stove. Paul had installed the large, rectangle chalkboard himself along one wall.

The State of Arizona paid her, meagerly, but she was dedicated all the same and worked many hours per day. Since Renee did not have a family of her own, she spent the most time prepping, grading and lesson planning. It was almost all she truly had in her life.

That was about to change after she met Sheriff Richmond and his daughter, Tabitha.

Prescott Temporary Grammar School, c. 1860

Sophia was wistfully staring out of one of the ceiling-high windows in her parlor. She sat upon the velvet settee, holding her second glass of champagne. Randolph, her husband, was still at the bank, late, as usual. Her taffeta and lace blue dress was the shade of her ice-blue eyes. Sapphires sparkled at her ears and neck. Her blonde hair was in an elaborate updo. Her dainty feet were clad in matching blue-silk low heels, each with a jewel that sparked under the overhead gold-gilded chandelier.

It was twilight, and Cape Cod in June was beautiful . . . warm, clear and teeming with blossoming peach and current trees as a result of a long cold winter. Perhaps it was the weather causing her feelings of an unsettledness.

She had just sent her daughter Tabitha on a 3,000-mile trek across the country and was second-guessing her decision to allow her to meet her father. She felt all at once unsure of her decision to let go of her daughter. Sophia sighed heavily as she remembered the early days of her marriage to Luke Richmond.

It had been a June day in Philadelphia, in 1874. She was living in her parents' home, and had just turned 21. She was thought by many to be one of the most beautiful young women in the whole of Pennsylvania State. She'd had suitors since she was sixteen, and they had left her wanting. Her mother also insisted that she choose her husband extremely carefully, and she would only allow her to marry if she approved of her daughter's choice.

Her mother, Margaret Ann York had been born in this very mansion twenty-five years earlier. Her mother's father was the Governor of the state at the turn of the 19th century, Thomas McKean. Wealth had begat wealth for at least four generations. But when Sophia met the tall, handsome rancher who was getting off the train that had traveled from Kentucky, she was intrigued.

He'd hopped off the train without using the step ladder while she was awaiting her sister Helena's return from boarding school in Massachusetts. He'd stopped to adjust the straps on his travel bag, and from behind him, her sister started down the steps carrying a parasol and her purse. It all happened so fast, Sophia had no idea how the tall stranger could have known, but suddenly she caught a heel in the lower step and started to fall. He spun around to catch her arm and righted her down to the ground. Her sister gasped loudly, and then tipped her head back and laughed, accepting his help.

"Oh, my goodness," she chirped, "I can't believe that!"

Luke held her hand a little longer before he pulled back and took off his wide-brimmed hat.

"Ma'am?" He looked down into her young, pretty face as she blushed a light pink.

"Oh, my goodness!" She repeated.

She had dropped her blue parasol on the ground, and he bent his knees to grab it and offer it to her.

She laughed as she accepted the polished, curved handle gently from his strong, tanned hand. Her white laced gloved hand gently touched his hand, and their eyes met. His grin was disarming, and she felt almost faint. Meanwhile, Sophia had quickly come to her side in panic.

"Helena, are you alright?!" Sophia set about fluffing out her sister's hem that was dusty, sighing and tsking. Helena laughed and laid her free hand on her sister's shoulder.

"Sophia! I'm perfectly fine...thanks to this kind gentleman!" Both women looked at Luke at the same time. The moment her blue eyes met his dark ones, he was entranced.

Her mouth was the color of a pink rosebud, and her cheeks were dusted with powder and slightly flushed. Her expression was at first puzzled, then, she blinked and a slow smile drew dimples at either side of her mouth. Her blonde hair was dazzling in the sunlight, and a golden locket graced her long, slim, milky neck.

Helena would have scowled if she'd had no manners, but she caught herself as she noticed the obvious interest in her older sister that the handsome man obviously felt, and instead, she impulsively hugged Sophia.

"Sophia! I'm so glad to be home! School was such a bore!" She quickly pulled back and stared at her. Sophia was still looking at the tall stranger, and the spell refused to be broken for the moment.

"Oh my...sir...I thank you for helping my sister!" Sophia slowly said, her smile widening. She put out her delicate hand, and Luke took it gently, and she pumped it up and down in a shake. He would have gladly kissed the back of her hand which felt soft and cool. He put his hat back on and smiled down at her.

"I'm glad I happened to be here to do so!" His voice was low and strong.

Helena asked, "And who might be you?" She stared up at him seriously.

"Luke Richmond. Pleased to meet you both!" He picked up his bag and extended his hand towards the platform of the station.

"Shall I walk you ladies back before there are any more near-accidents?" Both ladies bobbed their heads in nods and Luke let them lead, walking behind them away from the crowd to safety.

All three stood together as a train porter brought two large leather trunks to Helena.

"Where would you like these, Ma'am?" The young man cheerfully was happy to help such a pretty girl. She smiled charmingly at him.

"Oh yes, Sophia, did you bring the carriage?"

"Yes, I drove it myself, it's over there..." Sophia turned and pointed to a one-horse handsome four-wheeled carriage, with a beautiful quarter horse waiting patiently.

"Shall we?" Helena turned to Luke. "Surely we can take you somewhere?"

"Helena..." Sophie hesitated. "Mr. Richmond probably has someone waiting for him!"

She smiled politely at him, ever-conscious of proper etiquette drilled into her by her mother since she was young. Women are never to act forward with a man.

"Actually, I'm here to pick up a horse, so I need to wait here and take a train back home. May I escort you to your carriage?"

"Oh, well where is home Mr. Richmond?" Helena asked.

"Luke. Please call me Luke. It was Kentucky; Louisville to be precise. I'm moving out west presently. Do you both live here in Philadelphia?"

"Yes, we do." Helena answered. Sophia gave her a sharp look.

"Yes, and we should get to it, Mother will be waiting for us. Mr. Richmond, thank you again, Porter, please follow us if you will, Helena?" She looked at Luke one more time.

She felt a tug in her stomach, his dark eyes were friendly and kind. She had no idea who he was, or what he did for a living, but she had never been so attracted to any other man before meeting Luke Richmond.

"What kind of horse?" Helena didn't budge her position next to Luke.

"She's a Quarter Horse. She was my father's."

"Oh, I love Quarter horses!" Helena exclaimed.

"Yes, so do I." Sophia put her hand on Helena's shoulder. "Sister, we need to go now. Excuse us, Mr. Richmond."

Helena let Sophia lead, linking her arm into Luke's. The Porter followed them to their carriage and loaded the back. Luke helped them both into the front bench seat. He handed the reins into Sophia's hands and tipped his hat.

"Thank you again, Luke!" Helena flirted shamelessly, and adjusted her hat.

Sophia slapped the reins softly and the beautiful steed obediently stepped forward. They clip-clopped on soft dirt away from the station heading east.

Luke was sorry to see them go, her go, the beautiful blonde who held his hand moments ago, and was now riding away from him...would he ever see her again?

Luke Richmond, 1890

Her life today was good. She had raised Tabitha well and was pleased with her character, education and her full spirit. She was thoughtful of others, questioned everything, and the only area Sophia would like to change is her number of friends. She rarely talked about having friends at school, but she was content staying at home and studying and reading. She was usually sequestered in their grand library, and often discussed various topics with her stepfather. She never had shown any interest in boys. She was also an excellent horsewoman and would be a great beauty as she matured.

She never would have sent her west by herself had her daughter not given her every reason to trust her. Tabitha had a good head on her shoulder. Sophia smiled as she thought of the close relationship she had with her dog, Toby. She'd named him after the dog in Sir Arthur Conan Doyle's books. The popular new author who had written two novels about Sherlock Holmes, a London detective, held high interest for Tabitha, and she currently awaited a third book to be released. Sophia had read both novels after Tabitha finished them and enjoyed them immensely. Sophia had never had that closeness with the two Corgis she had delivered from London, her first home. Toby was actually Tabitha's best friend.

Sophia rose and helped herself to a third glass of the Bollinger champagne. She'd decided to trust her daughter completely and stop worrying. She anxiously awaited a first letter from her, and now, she awaited her husband's return from work with a renewed appreciation for his caring and love of her daughter. She eyed the antique English chime piece in the corner. Her husband was two hours late, again. She knew he'd have a credible excuse, but something had always pulled at her stomach as the late nights became more and more frequent.

Grandfather Clock, 1877, German

Tabitha was napping on the train bench, her head on the small pillow, dreaming about her last few moments in Philadelphia and the conversation her mother had with her in the parlor. She had known it would be about something serious, as her adoptive father Randolph sat next to Sophia and both were wearing serious expressions. She sat across from them on the apricot-colored silk chair with the ornate coffee table between them. The silver tea service had been set up on a tray.

"Darling, Randolph and I have decided to meet with you and talk about your father. This summer, I thought it a good idea for you to travel out west and spend some time with him. It's completely your choice, Tabitha. I...we thought you might be curious about where he lives, what he does as...the sheriff."

She pronounced the word slowly and carefully, as If the word was not in her vocabulary, allowing herself just a bit of snobbism to peek through, but subtle enough from years of politeness training not to offend. The law wasn't termed that way in the east. Police departments had been set up as law enforcement with more strict organization as time progressed. The country was nearing the start of the 20th century. Things were improving and getting more sophisticated as a result of modern living.

Tabitha didn't bat an eyelash. She looked at her step-father Randolph and he spoke softly.

"You are my adopted daughter, and I love you and care for you as if you were my own. Your mother and I thought this may be a good idea at this time. We trust you and know you will make the right decision about this. You can make it a short or long visit, entirely up to you."

He paused. "You are, after all, sixteen. You're a young lady now."

"How do you feel about it, honey?" Sophia gently asked.

Tabitha was silent, then she slowly and softly spoke.

"I have thought about him, I do have questions. I think it might be a fine idea, if I can take Toby with me? Would we ride on the train the whole way?"

"Oh yes, yes of course you can! And I think the train goes all the way to the ocean! Do you know Randolf?" Her father nodded.

"Yes, I believe it does now, I will check on that tomorrow. If there are any breaks in the track, we will make other transportation plans. We want you to get there safely. You will also have a contact along the way from the train company. All this will be precisely planned and you'll travel according to a strict itinerary."

"That all sounds proper."

Tabitha patted Toby, who sat at her feet curled up. He looked up at his mistress. "We're going to Arizona Territory, darling. You're coming with me. How do you like that?"

Toby cocked his head to the side, and eyed her as if he understood. He wagged his tail and she laughed.

"Ok, when do we leave?"

Tabitha Martin, 1890

Renee Boudreau stepped down from her buggy and tied up her Paint, Nicco, a gelding. She immediately went into the schoolroom to open up the windows, airing out the inside in the early-summer morning. She hefted her bag filled with heavy books and papers onto her desk. Outside, she unsaddled Nicco and led him into the back of the main building where his feed bucket and water was, under a lean-to awning that would shade him from the afternoon sun. It was 9:00 am when she was done with all her opening chores. She scratched on the chalkboard lesson plans for the three different levels she'd separated the 32-student class into. Primary and Secondary grades, as well as high school ages.

Her youngest student was a second grader; her eldest was fourteen. For upper grades, students had to attend Phoenix, Tucson or Mesa high schools. She oversaw the entire class. She preplanned group activities, taught them how to play games, and taught them about the world they lived in. They also worked on group projects. They grew succulents and learned about the Civil War. From different reference materials Renee could scramble to get her hands on, she made it as interesting a learning environment as possible.

Her brother Paul would help with repairs and landscaping around the building. He painted the outside, and set up the long tables in place of desks they could ill afford. He'd found the chalkboard somehow. He had also procured some playground equipment, like balls, rope for tug-of-war, and had plans to make a climbing structure.

It took all of her strength, energy and brain power to bring the school through from year to year, and she loved every minute of it. She was grateful for her brother's help when he was off the ranch where he now worked as Lead Ranch Hand. She felt that while she could have remained single forever and accepted that for the long haul, she wished for a nice woman for Paul to meet and make a life with.

She had yet to meet anyone who drew any real interest within. By this time in her mother's life, she had married and had two children. But with all she had to do, including teaching Bible lessons on Sundays, and cooking and cleaning the home they lived in, she had zero time for any socializing. Her brother Paul was just as busy if not more so than she, but she was not a substitute for a wife.

She would yearn for a good wife for her brother.

He would write songs, strumming on his guitar, and the words were poetry. It would be late at night before they turned in, and he would be sitting on one of the chairs on the porch. She would be cleaning up after dinner, wiping down the table, sweeping the floor. The front windows were open and the notes lilted into her, and she felt it was the most beautiful thing she'd ever heard. She'd smile to herself, put down the broom and come outside to take the other chair, not interrupting him. His gaze was on his fingers, pressing down on the guitar's frets. He had a happy look in his eyes that she'd never see except when he did this.

Paul would tell her the same thing...that she needed to find a good man, that she was too pretty to be alone, and she would just shake her head and softly laugh.

She noticed men looking at her in an over friendly manner, of tipping their hats when she passed by them in town, and it was nice that she was fair looking in her bedroom mirror, but there had been no tug at her heartstrings, as she had heard in one of Paul's songs, so she didn't spend days wistfully dreaming of meeting the right man or strong desire to let someone take care of her. It was off to the next task at hand. Little did she know that all this was about to change.

Guitar Song

She was the very last passenger to step down from the train car at the Yuma Train Station. Luke stood waiting and watching out for her, his hat in hand as passengers disembarked. It was 4:15, and the train was on time.

His breath was taken away. A lovely, red-haired beauty stood, with a white dog on a leash, and a small leather bag in her free hand. She squinted in the late afternoon sunlight, dressed in blue, looking around her before stepping delicately toward the platform, blue eyes shining bright and alert as to which greeter was her father. The station was very busy with people coming and going, and suddenly, he was staring into those eyes. He nodded, and a smile broke out on his face before he could help it.

She hesitated, and stared at him. She didn't smile. Her dog was glued to her side, and he dutifully stood at attention in the dust, staring up at him, perhaps appraising him too.

Her hair was the color of burnished copper. Her skin was a beautiful warm ivory. Her stature was erect, and she stood tall and slim. Her dress was definitely east coast style, and her hat was in her gloved hand. It looked to be straw with a blue ribbon. He was yanked back in time over sixteen years ago, when he held the hand of her mother.

They froze for a moment, until Luke said loudly, "Tabitha Martin?"

When she didn't respond, he stepped down from the wooden platform and slowly made his way towards her. He was about ten feet away now, but her white dog sprang into action and growled loudly, keeping his eyes on Luke.

He slowed his gait but the dog growling continued, low and menacing. Luke stopped about five feet in front of them. The dog started barking shrilly, until his mistress gently tugged the leash and said,

"Toby, no!" He immediately closed his mouth, but kept his standing position, not taking his eyes off of Luke.

"I'm Luke."

Tabitha nodded her head.

"I'm Tabitha"

The two politely shook hands.

"Thank you for meeting me. This is Toby, my English Terrier. He's very protective, so please keep your distance . . . at least for a while."

"Duly noted, ma'am." Luke put his hat on his head. "You have luggage?"

"Yes. A porter will be here shortly with my trunks." Luke nodded.

"Can I escort you to the platform until he comes?"

The two faced each other on the platform, and waited.

"So, I have a buckboard wagon, the going's a bit rough. I hope that's ok with you."

"Of course, I ride often."

"We'll stay the night tonight, then make our way to my ranch in Prescott."

"Very good. I need to change."

"Change?"

"Yes, into travel clothes."

"Travel clothes?" Luke was confused.

"Yes."

"You can use my room at the hotel."

"Thank you." Tabitha bent down to rub Toby down a bit.

"Where can we get water for him?"

"At the Livery Stables." Tabitha nuzzled Toby, and cooed to him. He responded with several kisses with his tongue to her cheek, but kept his eyes on Luke.

Finally, the porter came with two large leather trunks.

"Ma'am, your bags."

Tabitha reached into her purse and took out some coins, which she put into his hand.

"Thank you, sir." He eagerly accepted her gift, and quickly left the platform.

"Shall we?" Tabitha looked at Luke, who took a trunk in each hand. She was surprised at his obvious strength.

"Right this way!" He called over his shoulder, striding to the wagon he'd had tied up beside the station house. He was smiling as he strode. She was not a child; she was a young lady. She was his daughter.

19th Century Luxury Trunk

Paul was trotting his horse along the border of the west field, on fence detail, checking for downed posts and broken wire. Some settlers on the plains at this time resented ranchers that had erected barbed wire which injured their docile cattle. Before the influx of more ranchers in the west, there was an "open plain" policy, wherein the cattle owned by landowners could move around and graze a wide area. With ranchers buying up land and owning cattle farms, possessiveness took over to keep herds separate, thus changing the dynamics of a true "Wild West" era.

Native Americans felt their land was being sectioned off, bought, and taken by White Men, and would destroy fences and take any cattle for food that they could. Their buffalo resources had already diminished by 50%. They felt justified to take from the White Man what was comparable to what he had taken from them.

The farmers who had acres of crops, like wheat, corn, and other vegetables hated the barbed wire; there was no need to protect their crops. It was a threat to their right to settle there.

Paul would stop at the holes and use pliers and barbed wire and cutters to mend the holes. Sometimes whole panels from stake-to-stake were down. It took a lot of time. Even with his leather gloves he got cut. It was just part of the job. He liked his boss, liked the work, and liked being outdoors on a horse in open country. He was grateful for the work, living out west, and having a nice and comfortable home due to his sister's tender loving care.

He was older than her by two years, and had always looked out for her, and would continue to do so for the rest of his life. He sometimes worried about her being unmarried without children, with him as her only family, but she seemed content with her life the way things were. He would be fine without a wife and he was meant to work atop a horse outdoors, and basically be his own boss. His Pinto, the sire of his sister's horse, was true and strong. But he knew the sudden death of their parents had affected her more than him.

He intended to keep them safe and content in this Wild West territory that his parents had brought them to, without having conflict with any Natives. He was friendly to white men as well as red, or brown. He did not seek out trouble. But he knew he would fight to the death to protect what family he had left, if only his sister if necessary.

To keep him from getting lonesome on some long nights, he took his guitar and made melodies to his lyrics, written by lantern light after Renee fell asleep. He made up love songs as a way to sweeten the time. He remembered how loving his parents were towards each other and wished to remember it in song.

He hoped for a husband for Renee. But, she deserved the best, and he hadn't found the one for her, yet. He would keep looking, though. It was his job.

Ranch Worker

There was no one to contact. There was nothing to do but wait. She watched for the mail every day but still had no word from her darling girl. Sophia second guessed herself daily. Her husband was rarely home. She was bothered, and paced her parlor daily and nightly. She was drinking more wine than usual and she didn't see a way out of her angst.

She wondered if she should have gone with her daughter out west. She wondered if she should have left Arizona Territory at all. She didn't have any real friends to be able to talk to, but knew she must do something.

What if her daughter remained away? What if she found her father more desirable to be around, to live with, to share secrets with about her?

She looked around her ornately decorated parlor, lit by a crystal chandelier, with silk and velvet upholstered furniture, teak-wood trimmings and Persian rugs upon polished maple-wood flooring. Her windows were sparkling, her wood was dusted, her silver was polished and any glassware was cleaned to a shine.

Her clothing was ordered from France, London and New York fashion houses. Her hats were imported. Her shoes were Italian. Her jewelry was from the best shops in town, set in platinum, with sapphires and diamonds. Her baths were drawn for her in a large porcelain tub in her own private bathroom, with wall-sized mirrors and plush towels. She was waited on, catered to and well taken care of. She needn't leave the house, ever, with the number of servants that were now paid to tend to her every need.

Sophia Mary York Richmond Martin was without a true friend in the world. All acquiesced as a duty to her. It was their job to help her, do the task and step away. They desired no more time with her than that. In social circles it was also the wives of her husband's peer's duty to politely smile, agree with and respect her position in the community. She received daily invitations to a myriad of parties, soirees, weddings, baptisms and annual balls. Fundraisers for various charities required attendance at their level of the elite.

It left her feeling quite lonely. Especially with her husband being gone most hours of the day. She'd met the banking staff several times when she'd accompanied Randolph from time to time. There were several men, and few women who worked for him, but one woman had stood out to her. It was a young dark-haired lady in rather form-fitting dresses who fairly gazed after her President of Operations husband. She seemed always to always be at his elbow, completing some tasks for him, acting demure and never uttering a word while his wife was present.

Sophia knew her personal power of beauty and grace. She knew Randolph had been very attracted to her in their early years of a relationship, quickly asking her to marry him and offering her a life of leisure and travel. But she was now forty years old, and there were younger, more beautiful women in his world. She'd not been able to grant him a son or daughter of his own for no reason that she knew. Perhaps he desired that, not that he ever articulated this. They'd never discussed it. She'd just never gotten pregnant, and he seemed to truly love Tabitha, her daughter by her first marriage to Luke.

Her husband hadn't touched her sexually in over one year. At present, they slept in separate bedrooms. She assumed, or let herself believe, that because he was going to run for Mayor of New York in the next election year, he was very focused on everything that was necessary to carry that out. Sophia, however, was aware of how her mother managed her marriage. She'd appeared with her husband at many social functions as much as possible. But their marriage was loveless. That was one of the reasons she couldn't wait to move west and get away from her home. And she swore her marriage would never be like her mother's. And yet, here she was . . .

Sophia was less interested in keeping up this facade. Perhaps she needed to put herself out there more, rejoin some of the women's clubs she'd been a part of upon her marriage. She could start a new charitable organization in New York City and Chair the board. But she would in time grow bored, as she did at the few functions she did attend.

She could shop more in the stores on main streets instead of ordering privately from Europe. Her mother had turned to private vendors, rather than mingle with "common folk" and walk among people on dirt streets and wooden aisles in small stores with only limited supplies, usually catering to local styles.

She didn't know what to do at the moment, but for now, she spent the evening alone in her parlor, reading several newspapers about news from the west and how the economy was growing in ranching, mining and farming. Her interest was piqued. She started thinking seriously about widening her horizons beyond the eastern seaboard. She started cutting out articles.

Wild West News

He stood alone, as he often did, arms crossed in front of him, feet apart, eyes focused on the distant sunset in the beautiful

Sonoran Desert, his home. He wore deerskin breeches, no shirt, buffalo moccasins. He wore a silver medallion on a silver chain around his neck. His long coarse straight hair fell down his back, slightly ruffling in the warm breeze. He stood still for several minutes, thinking over the days behind him and the days ahead. Aditsan had many things on his mind.

His father, leader of their tribe two decades ago, had instructed him as the new leader to take only one day at a time to plan, to review, and to decide on an action to keep the tribe safe. Letting worries flood one's peace of mind would not be productive. The tribe counted on its chief. His job is to keep the entire community safe. He must earn their trust. Everyone must believe in him, no matter what. They must be willing to give their lives for him to protect the others. For that, a leader needed great peace of mind.

Watching the greater communities of the Navajo, his people, dwindling each year that went by with the influx of the White Man was complicated. The Chief must outrun his own thoughts of anguish, anger, sadness, revenge, fear and panic. He must find a way to survive and fight. It was difficult in his father's time, with the rising of the Apache Nation in many pre-Civil War conflicts, and now with the expansion of mining, farming and ranching. In his experience, the White Man almost always told lies. He wanted to take their food, their water, their land and their spirit. He wanted to take down the Red Man and take over all the power for themselves. The Red Man thought of his community first in all things; the White Man thought only of himself.

His father would go for hours on long treks with Aditsan, leading him to a high place, a hill, a mountain. They would listen to the wind in stillness, not talking. Aditsan's very name meant, "Listener". His father would begin teaching when he was ready, which could be after as long as an hour of silence. He taught his son the importance of listening to nature, which you can only hear if you are a good listener, saying nothing. Nature spoke first in the world. Animals spoke second. Man spoke third. He had much more to listen to.

The missionaries who arrived in the beginning of the 19th century taught natives their alphabet, in English, and the Navajo used most of these letters to write down their "tones", which were four different ways of speaking: low, high, rising and falling. Some words were written down in exactly the same way, the meanings changing according to the tone of the word spoken. Navajo written language used 23 out of the English 26 letters, excluding u, v and x. There are several vowels strung together in some words, and each has a different tone.

So complex is the Navajo tongue that it would be used in the 20th century during World War II as a code to speak while broadcasting via walkie-talkie that could not be understood by anyone except those few Navajo that knew the language. That would then be translated to the American soldiers and never be understood by Japanese or German forces.

All this was moot for Aditsan, for he rarely spoke and had never read the language in print, which was not known to have been scribed at this time in history. 1958 would be the first official Navajo-English Dictionary in print.

There were few men he spoke to using his language, only his people. He knew Apache, and there was only one White Man he'd spoken to in Navajo. He had met one of the White settlers whom he respected and could tolerate for any length of time. There was no fear or tension between this man and him. And this was because this man saved him and his family's life years before. And for this, Aditsan gave the gift of one of his best horses...a certain Appaloosa mare, a foal of his father's stallion two generations past.

It was time for a trek south from his home in Rock Point in NE Arizona Territory to the Yavapai Nation where his friend lived. He would bring two of his warriors, his brothers. They would avoid Apache areas further SE. They would set out at night and he would meet up with this man, his friend, who went by the American name, Richmond.

Southward Vista

Luke Richmond and Tabitha Martin arrived in Prescott during the evening, and drove up the dirt drive up to the large two-story house. The wagon team came to a stop and Luke bounced down to the ground to unload the leather trunks and take them into the house. Tabitha carefully stepped down to the ground and looked around her. She was wearing tan culottes, wide-leg trousers that looked more like a skirt. A blue silk long sleeved blouse, black dress boots, and black leather gloves.

The sun was just setting, and she couldn't clearly see everything, but the house appeared to be well-tended and it wasn't at all what she had imagined. Luke had lit the gas lamp in the parlor and the light cast a gentle warmth across the room.

Inside, the home was pleasant, and Luke called from the second floor,

"I put your things up here."

He came down the stairs.

"Your room is on the left of the staircase."

She nodded, looking up at him, holding Toby's leash.

"I have to take the wagon back to Cliff. It won't take long, are you hungry?"

Tabitha shook her head.

"Just thirsty."

Luke lit another lamp in the dining room.

"The kitchen's through there. There's well water you can draw from the sink. Help yourself to whatever you'd like."

He looked at her for a whole minute as she put down her small leather tote in the entryway. They'd driven a long way together, with only perfunctory conversation. She'd been so quiet, not complaining about the roughness of the roads, polite. They ate from food he'd packed. They stayed in a small inn half way along, she on the bed, him in his saddle bag bed on the floor.

She asked him no questions, and Toby had stopped growling at him. She'd tended to his needs completely, treating him as if he were a child. It was charming, and she was disarming. He hadn't known what kind of challenge it would be to form some kind of relationship with her, but he was willing to try and get to know his daughter.

She made her way into the kitchen, and he moved to show her how to light the gas lamp but she did it herself. It made her skin glow brightly as the darkness of night fell. Luke left her to it, and went out the door to make the exchange with his neighbor and ride Charlotte home.

When he had put his horse in the barn with fresh hay and wiped her down, he returned to the house to find her bedroom chamber door closed. He went to his chamber and undressed and got into bed. He, as she, hit the pillow and went right out. A blessed, restful sleep was just what they needed for what lay ahead for them both.

Gas Lamp, 1890

It was a beautiful sunny morning Sunday, and Luke quietly went about his morning routine, not wanting to wake up Tabitha. He was not obliged to go into work today, and thought he could show her around the small ranch and perhaps take a ride around the area. He started the coffee and looking through his pantry he was sorry he hadn't bought food supplies. He, of course, hadn't known what she would like, but he could have gotten the basics.

The ice box was empty and he needed to get another block of ice so they could store meat and milk, butter and eggs. He would make a run to the grocery for supplies. Perhaps she would go with him. She could ride Bandit, his other horse. He'd only had Charlotte since after he met

Aditsan, about three years ago. She was faster than Bandit, and younger. Bandit was a draft horse, and had more power.

He didn't know anything about his daughter, what she liked, what she was used to. Was he a total idiot for thinking that he could take this on? She wore fancy clothes, high heels, ribbons in her hair, high-class bags, even a dog for God's sake! What had he gotten himself into!?

He sighed loudly, and poured black coffee into his mug. It smelled good and strong, and after his quick bath this morning, he'd put on fresh clothes. He'd even shaved his grown-out beard, leaving his mustache.

He rubbed his chin, and sighed again. What must he appear like to her? Did he look like some backwards cowboy? If so, how did he expect her to fit in, clearly an eastern-raised young lady, conditioned to more refined living. He looked up the stairway where she slept in her chamber. Was she already packing up to leave?

He turned, gazing out the window. It would do him no good to speculate. He would just have to take it one day at a time. First things first. He drained his cup and picked up his work gloves on the table by the door and stepped outside.

He would saddle the horses, and get ready to ride with . . . his daughter.

His small barn boarded his two horses, tools, bales of hay and crates of various items in storage. The ranch was a previous homestead settled 30 years prior. He'd purchased it from the money he'd been left by his parents, who raised him in Kentucky on a horse farm. His father raised thoroughbreds, and his mother was a serious horsewoman. He'd been an only child. He'd not gone to college, but had instead learned their trade. When he was 20, his parents passed away and while he wanted to carry on and run the place after them, he found he was too young and without any support to help him to continue running the farm, and ended up being advised to sell out and start a new life.

He'd heard about expansion in the west, and asked people about their opinion of his starting up out there. His parents' friends helped him find out specific information through their friends, newspapers and others. One of those friends was in law enforcement, and told Luke there was a great need for residents in low-populated areas of different territories, and with the growing population, law enforcement officials would be imperative. Would he be interested in being set up with a place to live and be appointed to a position? This is what he asked himself over and over again. He was still so young, but he was also very adventurous in spirit, and with his parents sadly gone, he held no allegiance to his home of birth.

A certain friend of his father told him there was a horse in Philadelphia that belonged to his father, and needed to be picked up and taken possession of. It would be a useful horse for him, a Draft gelding only a year old by name of Bandit. That was when Luke made his decision to head out west. He only had to pick up the horse and ride out after sending his possessions out ahead of him. And that was when he met his wife, who'd had his child, who was now living with him.

Bandit

Luke heard the dual whinnies as he opened the barn door and slid the opposite door on its pulleys to create a wide opening. He went first into Bandit's stall, rubbing his nose, greeting him after being away for four days. Cliff had checked on his feed and water, or had his sons do so, and he looked in good spirits with his master home. He spoke to him low and softly, and rubbed him down with his gloved hands down his side and over his flanks. He led him out to the great area covered with hay on the floor and made sure to flake off fresh hay from a bale with the pitchfork.

He then greeted Charlotte, rubbing her back and flanks, and leading her out to join Bandit with another flake of fresh hay. On leads secured by the railing of the stalls, he readied to saddle and rein the two up for the ride with his daughter.

He knew Bandit was tame and a good fit for Tabitha. They had briefly discussed her riding capabilities on the trip home, and she simply said she could ride a western saddle. She had also ridden a side saddle and English. Her stepfather owned a stable with thoroughbreds and her horse Pomegranate was stabled there. She had competed in Dressage competitions and was quite skilled, but had only shared minimally with him. He would soon see she had been modest.

Luke slowly led the horses to the tie up at the rail outside the barn. He would muck the stables that evening. He didn't want to dirty his clothes. He liked having his hand in caring for his animals. He had dreams of having more horses, but was too preoccupied with his sheriffing. For now, he was content. He took to brushing them before saddling them up with slow, deliberate strokes causing them to whinny in anticipation of a ride.

Horse brush; curry brush

Tabitha had awakened very early, before she heard Luke trying to quietly walk down the hall and staircase. After he'd gone downstairs, she quietly rose on bare feet and padded around her chamber. She entered the washroom in the hall to wash her face and brush her teeth. She brushed her hair 100 times as she'd done every morning and evening of her life. She braided it again, down her back. She applied her face cream and excitedly dressed in her room in a new outfit she'd bought without her mother's permission or knowing. It was a women's western gear outfit, for the same purpose as she'd worn the eastern style habit for riding.

It was a white blouse with pearl buttons down the front and at the cuffs. Soft, buttery leather of a tanned color breeches tucked into tall boots, and a new leather belt with silver buckle cinched them at the waist. There were no zippers at this time, only buttons and clasps, and these buttoned up at the side. She had no idea what hat would match her outfit, so went without. She started downstairs with butterflies flitting in her stomach. This was the first time she'd ever worn anything but a skirt or a dress. What would her mother think? She smiled, and made her way into the kitchen.

It was empty, and she smelled the coffee. Helping herself to a black cup, which she'd never had before either, liberally adding cream and sugar as her mother did, she thought it tasted different from her usual tea but good. She caught her reflection in the huge full-length mirror in the entryway and stopped at her first look at her whole outfit. She gasped, ...tossing her head back. Her light blue eyes sparkled. She carried her cup and wandered outside onto the porch. A wooden eave covered it, and she gazed out onto the land before her that was fenced in on all three sides.

The air was fresh and mild. She eyed the country from left to right, where she spied her father tending to two beautiful horses, swinging their tails and snorting, as if ready to go and waiting for her. Joy filled her heart which beat faster at this freedom she felt of being somewhere new, strange, and so far away from her home. She stood quietly and stared at her father until he looked up and stopped his work.

Luke looked up towards the house casually, and saw her, standing there, and at that moment decided he'd done exactly the right thing in bringing her here. She looked lovely, without the trappings of some ornate costume, wearing actual breeches and a practical blouse. She was beautiful, and a lovely child that he had helped make. It was unbelievable the feeling inside of him that planted itself in his heart and would grow daily as the relationship formed between them. But for now, he could only stand in awe of her. He was speechless.

She stepped down the three steps from the porch and joined him, putting her hand on Bandit's neck and giving him some rubs. He whinnied and nosed her hand, pushing it towards her, wanting more attention. She smiled, looking into the horse's deep brown eyes, and said,

"He's a beauty! What's his name?" Luke came out of his trance and answered,

"He's Bandit."

"Morgan?"

"Close, Mogan-Draft."

Luke was impressed. Draft horses have all kinds of strains and blood, which made them great work horses. Quarter horses and Draft breeds are often a good mix. She called it right.

"Now this Appaloosa, she's Charlotte.

Tabitha switched to greet her, and while she was more aloof than Bandit and did not invite more attention, keeping wide dark eyes on her, she remained calm under the watchful eye of her Master.

"I've never stood this near one. Beautiful!"

She smiled widely. Luke gave her a brush and she finished brushing Bandit, as he curried Charlotte.

"Am I dressed appropriately?" Luke nodded.

"Yes ma'am. I didn't know what you would be riding in, but your dresses might be a bit...uncomfortable...out here. Not many...paved roads."

She laughed.

"I haven't seen any yet! Where are we going?"

"I thought I'd show you around the area, are you up to it?"

"Yes I am."

He took her brush and disappeared into the barn and came back with his large saddle bag to pack with groceries. He strapped it behind Bandit's saddle, and turned to her.

"May I help you saddle up?"

She shook her head.

"I think I can manage. I would like to buy some riding gloves too."

He cocked his head.

"And a proper hat."

He smiled as he untied her horse's reins and stood ready to hand them to her once she was atop. She smoothly slipped her booted left foot into the stirrup and glided into the saddle, perfectly. He handed her the reins which she took lightly into her hands. Bandit stepped around a bit, but decided he would carry her tamely.

Luke saddled up on his horse, and Charlotte pranced in place, anxious to get going.

"You ready?" He yelled.

"Yes!" She held her own sidling up next to him.

He needn't press his boots into her, as she reacted immediately, easily loping down the dirt drive to the road. Tabitha did not have to even urge her horse forward, as

Bandit automatically followed his Master for his new Mistress.

Luke led for their first mile of riding, then slowed to ride side-by-side with his daughter. Again, he was impressed. The way she carried herself in the saddle and moved with the horse was fluid. He couldn't believe he actually asked her if she could ride. She looked like she had been born riding. What else would she surprise him with? He found himself smiling naturally as he rode. And she was his daughter . . .

He had them stop at different places along the way. The end of his property, his neighbor's ranch, pointing to Mingus Mountain, and the direction of Watson Lake which they would go to another day. They passed the many pines and cottonwoods that were thick on either side of them, and she noted they started traveling uphill. Luke had mentioned that they were "The Mile High Town" in elevation, and that in December, January and February it snowed several feet here.

She was used to winter snow, having lived in New York, but snow in the city she would see is much different than in the wide, high desert, and she looked forward to experiencing it. Her attendance at one of the esteemed eastern colleges had been left up in the air with her parents, and she was grateful she hadn't agreed to anything before she'd traveled here. It was difficult to even let thoughts of home creep into her mind set, as she smelled the pine trees, felt the warm, late-spring sun, caught sight of the perfect blue sky, and felt the horse beneath her that she was learning to handle perfectly as they rode, and she felt his response to her legs' pressure.

They walked the horses for a while, then loped them again, and reached Prescott Town in about half an hour. They let them graze in some pasture land half-way.

They talked about what she liked to do back east, and what his sheriff's job entailed. She was easy to talk to, and he felt a bond beginning between them. He liked traveling, even if just to town with a companion. He was used to doing everything on his own. Her company was the most interesting he'd ever experienced.

As they came up to the main street which was named Gurley Street, after the first Governor of the Arizona Territory, there were buggies drawn by carriages traveling both ways on the wide street. It was flanked with many buildings, businesses and railings for horses.

Luke pointed to and explained businesses along the road. He led them to his office, a stone and wood building with a large sign SHERIFF hung over the large entryway. They tied up their horses at the railing in front.

"Over there where that construction crew is working, that will be the first City Hall Plaza building Prescott's had."

Tabitha eyed the wagons and men in a massive leveled area and the framework for a three-story building. The noises and conversation carried over to them. She felt in such a different realm than in her crowded city at home. It was so spread out, and the new building will look so foreign among the clapboard and facade structures now lining the street. It truly looked like one of the many magazine and newspaper photos she poured through days before.

Luke walked side-by-side by his daughter up the steps and entered through the wooden doors. Upon entry, his two deputies stood up behind their wooden desks in the front entryway smiling.

"Good morning, sir!" they both said at once.

They were young men, dressed in khaki button down shirts with small silver badges tucked into jeans, wearing boots. Luke smiled as he noted their formality, he supposed in the presence Tabitha, and easily replied,

"At ease, guys. This is my...daughter, Tabitha. Tabitha, these are my deputies, Deputy Calvin and Deputy Johnson."

She smiled and bobbed her head at them both.

"Good morning." They nervously replied,

"Good morning, Ma'am!" again in unison.

Luke almost laughed.

"Uh, any news boys?"

Both men nodded. Calvin answered,

"A couple things, but no emergencies. Notes are on your desk."

"Ok, I'm showing Tabitha around town, so I'll leave it to you men!"

He led her into the back room, which was his small office, and an entry into the black-barred cells where offenders were held. She looked around the sparse room, not venturing into the back room.

He had one window and a desk and chair. Piles of papers were set atop his desktop, and two chairs were in front of his desk. There was a clock on the wall.

He sat at the desk as she waited, and looked through what he found on top, grunting a couple of times, then looking up.

"Nothing to be tended to today. How about breakfast?"

She nodded, and he rose to lead the way out, saying a quick goodbye to the boys.

They walked about 10 minutes down the street, leaving the horses behind. He chatted about the town, and how it was growing, about the City Hall building going up next to them, and how it was going to become a huge plaza, with trees on a green lawn surrounding a stately building where he would eventually move into.

She remained silent, listening to his steady voice, speaking familiarly with her about his home with some pride. It wasn't crowded on the streets, and the people she saw walking were dressed very plainly, but those who met Luke's eyes said polite hellos.

The Palace Restaurant & Saloon was the first of many more future eating establishments right in the center of the town. The ceiling was extraordinarily high with low-hung oil lamps. A huge area in the center of the dining area was a sky light, which let in streaks of sun rays so there was no need for lamps inside. It was very crowded this Sunday, near twenty patrons dining with bustling waitresses tending to them.

The aroma upon their arrival made her stomach growl, and an attractive lady came up to them quickly, smiling widely at her father.

"Heh, Sheriff! Nice to see you!" She had her dark hair piled high on her head. She wore a simple dress with a white apron tied around her trim waist. Luke nodded.

"And you, Mary. Well, we need a table for two!" She eyed Tabitha, and looked appreciatively at his daughter.

"Yes, sir! Follow me!"

She led them into the spacious area in between the tables; a long bar where some men stood drinking was to the left. A newsstand and sundry shop were near the front. Along the walls, booths that seated four with benches for seats had high wooden backs to separate them.

As they crossed the wooden floor, a few people noticed Luke and said hello, and definitely looked at her with curiosity. He would say hello back, and the two were led to a booth and sat across from each other.

Mary handed them her paper menus and beckoned a waitress over to their table.

"Mary, meet my daughter, Tabitha! She just arrived yesterday from New York!"

Her eyes grew wide and she looked at the young lady with kindness, studying her face with interest.

"Well, aren't you a unique beauty for these parts, my dear. Welcome to The Palace!"

After they ordered they sat looking at each other in silence. Then Luke started to grin, and chuckled.

"I have no idea what to ask you, but I have a thousand questions . . . at least. How about you?"

Tabitha nodded and smiled back. Bright eyes flashed a knowing look that she got his meaning. Then her face took on a serious effect.

"Did you ever know I existed before this?"

Luke waited before he answered her.

"I received a letter from . . . your mother two months ago. She told me you would be coming out here to meet me. She said to take good care of you. Before that, I knew nothing. And . . . I haven't heard from her since she left in 1874."

Silence passed between the two. He asked,

"How long have you known about me?"

"My mother told me when I was 12 years old. We went to tea at The Carlisle and she calmly told me I had a father who lived in a western territory. She told me she was married to you, but needed to return home to her parents. She didn't go into any details. I researched the area she said you were living in, but never knew how to contact you. She did not want any communication between herself and you, and that included me. I . . ."

She took a sip of water. Luke waited patiently.

"I wasn't angry with her; I don't know if I should be. I just . . . think she wanted what was best for me, and didn't want my life and education interrupted, until I was older."

"I . . . I was very angry at her, when she left."

Luke began slowly.

"I can't remember that now, but after I received her letter, I didn't feel angry, I could only think about what it would be like to meet you. You are . . . amazing. I am . . . in awe of you."

Tabitha was struck by his words and almost felt like crying. Their food arrived and she was starving, as neither of them had had dinner the night before.

Her father had bacon, eggs, and potato cakes. She ordered scrambled eggs with fruit and toast. It tasted delicious, and she finished every bite. They didn't speak in between chews and it was one of the most delicious meals she'd ever eaten.

They finished, and after Luke greeted a few more patrons, they walked back to the station.

"Let's ride to the grocery and load up on supplies, then we can go a way back near Mingus Mountain area. It's pretty country. Bandit can handle the load."

They rode to the Grocery and Mercantile which were connected. They shopped for what they needed, and more. Tabitha stepped down into the spacious Mercantile and looked at local clothing, hats, gloves, and women's accessories. She bought some leather gloves and Luke suggested a western-style hat that matched the same shade as her breeches. She liked his choices. He insisted on treating her on her first shopping trip.

As her purchases were being wrapped, Tabitha noticed a smartly dressed woman. She had on a white blouse and wore sand-colored breeches with a leather belt, and wore her blonde hair short. She was studying something at the front counter. She carried a tote that held some items. She wore short black boots, and had a commanding voice as she questioned the merchant behind the counter, pointing to the thick book she was flipping through. Tabitha had never seen a grown woman wearing her hair so short. She fingered her very long braid slowly.

Satisfied with their purchases, Luke loaded up the bags behind Bandit's saddle, and led them toward home, by way of the mountain, which was covered with large rocks and pine trees. Their horses stepped carefully on the rough terrain. It was beautiful country and they enjoyed following a trail that wound around the base to view the desert from 360 degrees.

Luke again was impressed with her handling of Bandit, stepping over stones and around boulders. They let the horses graze as they sat to view the northern vista, where the San Francisco Peaks jutted up to 7,000 feet in elevation and were no longer snow capped. The weather had changed that quickly in time after days of bright sunshine. Summer was just around the corner and outdoor activities would be part of daily life.

In July there would be the annual Town Independence Parade and Bar-b-que. A dance at the Rodeo Grounds was followed by three days of the Prescott Rodeo, a County Fair, and hopefully a peaceful coexistence with the Natives and Mexicans.

They arrived home, unloaded the supplies, and Luke tended the horses as Tabitha put away their purchases and started organizing the kitchen. She'd never managed the cooking in her home, but she intended to find out how to. She looked for a recipe book in the drawers and in the pantry, without success. She made a mental note to purchase one.

After a simple dinner, she went with her father to put the horses in for the night. They brushed them down, gave them fresh well water and made sure they had clean hay in their stalls. Luke had mucked when they'd gotten home but he told her she could help the next night. She willingly agreed.

They sat together on the porch, on the bench Luke had fashioned himself. They sat silently and watched another beautiful sunset in the quiet, darkening desert.

"How do you like it here so far?" Luke rather shyly asked.

"I like it very much. I need to learn a few things, but, I think...this...my coming out here...was a good idea...do you?"

"Yup." Luke looked at her beside him.

They both sat in silence, listening to crickets sing their happy "yups" too.

Richmond Ranch, c. 1880

Monday was usually the beginning of the school week for most children in Prescott, but this week was the first week of summer vacation, the first week of June, 1890. Her job was now to clean up the classroom, store many materials, and clean the tables and floor. She had submitted her grades to the Arizona Territorial Education District which was located in Phoenix and everyone was being promoted to the next grade. She also put out flyers for when the next school year starts, and she would travel to outer areas to meet families in person and talk to them about enrolling their children. Many did not have transportation; others needed all hands on deck to help with farms and ranches. Yavapai was a large area with small communities dotted far and wide. Renee often brainstormed about a way to reach all children, at least the younger ones for whom the basics were imperative to learn so the older children could help out at home.

With more settlers arriving in groups, Renee anticipated having a larger class of students in the fall, and so wanted to prepare for that, so making more room somehow for two separate classes, which would mean hiring another teacher would be necessary. It took a lot of time, questions, and patience. Also, she wanted to put in a request for new materials she would need to start the next year appropriately. It was not going to be a vacation for her, and yet she enjoyed the business of organizing and preparing. She would count on Paul to help with some of the bigger projects she had on her list of "to do's."

Eventually she would desire her own independent classroom building and always kept an eye out for any possibilities in town, or in the surrounding areas, but it was never possible with funds she couldn't yet procure. It would take many donations, from individuals and local businesses. She was always seeking out a solution for the many hurdles she'd faced over her years of teaching. She never ran out of enthusiasm. It wasn't her nature to give up, or even to complain.

She sat at her desk that morning looking over the list she'd taken to the Mercantile in town to order supplies yesterday. Their inventory was limited, so she could order from the Phoenix stores that had more inventory and choices of what she could purchase by catalog. She crossed off what she had bought the day before.

Classroom Needs	Building Needs
Erasers (6)	Tables, chairs cleaned
Chalk (6 boxes)	Mop floors
Pencils (3 boxes 5 w/ erasers)	**Repainting??
Lined tablets (4 reams, 24 each)	Window cleaning
Leveled readers [10 ea. Level (8 levels)]	**Repair sink faucet
Inkwells w/pens (20 sets)	**Fix cracked porcelain sink
Art paints/paper/brushes (20 ea.)	Clean wood stove, ice box
Color crayons (20 boxes)	
Leveled workbooks Reading, Writing, Math (50 ea.)	**Ask pastor John for help??
Additional Textbooks R, W, M??	Clean oil lamps, restock oil and wicks
Pencil sharpeners (2)	

Renee could have made pages of materials she hoped to be able to acquire for her teaching, but she started with the basics. She'd left the school hopeful as she led her horse pulling the wagon downtown so that she could fulfill at least some items on her shopping list.

Renee Boudreaux

It was just for a moment in time, but it was memorable, for them both. It was very ordinary, happenstance, nothing to even give a thought to. But it happened, for them both.

They were both shopping, Renee and Luke, at the Mercantile. Up at the payout counter, their elbows grazed each other. and their eyes met. Luke smiled and nodded his head. She smiled too, then a loud crashing sound caused everyone to freeze in place for a second or two. A young girl had accidently knocked over something glass in the center of the room, and it lay on the floor in pieces. Her mother excitedly started to chide her daughter, who ducked her head, eyes frozen on the floor. Renee was compelled to put down her tote and walk over to the embarrassed girl.

"Betty! Are you ok?"

She put a comforting hand on the girl's shoulder, who looked up at Renee, recognizing her.

"Do you know how many times I've knocked over something in a store?" Renee shook her head and laughed.

"June! Nice to see you!"

The mother, June, looked embarrassed, and gave a nervous laugh.

"Oh, Miss Boudreau! I... didn't see you!"

She took the hand of her daughter and pulled her over to her side.

"I... bet you are glad it's summer! Are you taking a trip somewhere?"

"Oh no, I'll be tending to things here! But I'll miss Betty! She is one of my favorite students!"

"Oh, my!" June blushed, and both women looked up as a young man neared them with a sweeper and pan.

"Pardon me, ladies, I'll just get this cleaned up."

He was in an apron, and he quickly swept the glass pieces away.

"Well, I guess I better see about that vase!"

She smiled at the teacher and quickly whisked her child away. Renee looked after them, then returned to the counter where Tabitha and her father were paying for their purchases. Renee retrieved her tote bag and made her way out the door, but stopped to say hello to Mr. Andrews, the father of her student Joshua. Tabitha and her father made their way out too, and all three met at the door at the same time.

Man and woman brushed elbows, this time harder, this time Luke turned to the short-haired woman and said,

"I'm sorry...again..." They both met eyes and both let out a laugh. This was their second encounter.

Luke tipped his hat and led Tabitha towards their horses. Renee turned in the opposite direction towards her wagon. She awaited one of the merchants to carry out two boxes for her. It had been a successful trip, and she'd ordered other things from the new catalog. She smiled as she received her goods, and then made her way into the grocery next door. She wanted to make an extra-special dinner. As she waited to be served, a certain pair of blue eyes came into her mind. How funny to run into him twice within a few minutes after never seeing him before.

Renee thought about those blue eyes, the tall handsome man with apparently his teenage daughter, both strangers to her, but still...memorable. The young lady's beautiful red hair stood out. But those eyes...

As Luke saddled up and Tabitha sidled up beside him as they turned homeward, he couldn't forget those warm, deep-brown eyes with long long lashes underneath a mane of short golden hair. He'd never seen her before, would he again?

Luke Richmond

It was early morning, and Tabitha turned over onto her back in bed and stretched fully. The sun was up, a breeze floated in through her slightly open window. She lay still and thought about her big first day out west. She smiled as she reviewed the photos in her mind of the places, people and feelings she'd experienced. But it was really about how easy it had been meeting her father, when she had had no expectations. It had been such an effortless connection. He naturally, it seemed, made her feel comfortable, welcome, even in such an unfamiliar territory. He didn't treat her as a stranger. He treated her as if she'd been coming for visits all her life.

Another photo she examined more carefully.

She'd never seen a grown woman with short hair before. Everyone back east wore their hair long or in an updo. All her girlfriends had curled tresses and ponytails with ribbons and bows. But the blonde woman in the store who was dressed in breeches stood out, as did her commanding voice when she stepped in to rescue the little girl from being scolded by her mother in public. Her dark eyes, from what Tabitha barely saw, were warm and kind. From her understanding of the conversation that the girl and she had had, the lady was a teacher.

She was curious about her. She wondered if her father knew her. She yawned, pushed back her covers, and started her day.

Luke was up early, as usual, and would be working that day. He wasn't sure how to handle Tabitha's day, but he was sure she was capable of working it out. He smiled as he tucked in his uniform shirt with his Sheriff badge pinned on into his jeans. He made up his bed and made his way down the hall, pausing at Tabitha's door. He stood to listen to see if she was up, but couldn't hear anything yet. He continued down the hall and downstairs.

Starting up the coffee in the kitchen, he heated the metal coffee pot filled with water on the gas stove. He went out onto the porch and sat on the bench. Stretching out his legs, he gazed out upon the sunlit morning. It felt like about 80 degrees already, so summer had arrived, unofficially. He thought about his day ahead.

He would catch up with anything at the office, make his usual Monday stops to businesses and deal with any walk-in traffic. Calvin would have the next two days off, so Johnson would be with him and make stops too. There were orders of supplies to pick up at the Livery, Mercantile, Grocery, and Lumber Yard. Literally, these businesses used these titles under which they did business, but licenses for ownership is something he would help them with by being a liaison with the State. He also was in charge of making sure taxes were paid by residents registered on the 1880 census, and he would be managing the conducting of the new decade census being taken shortly.

He had a lot of duties, and also took on many he wasn't officially in charge of. He wanted to do his best in uniting this community. But his goal was to make a start on running his own horse ranch for breeding and training quality stock. He would need time, help, and the best horse handlers he could find.

1875 was the very first run of the Kentucky Derby, and his father's stock was certainly a part of that sensational happening, then and past years since. The Richmond name was well-known in equine circles back east.

His parents had left him very well off, and with the sale of the farm, he had quite a savings put away. But he was very careful with his holdings and had disciplined himself to spend his money carefully to be able to put together the kind of operation he'd dreamed of.

And now, he had someone to leave it to...the beautiful young lady who now lived with him. He could tell she shared in his love of horses innately as a part of her. It made him smile, now, and he heard her come downstairs. Soon she made her way out to the porch with a cup in her hand. She smiled.

"Good morning, Tabitha. How did you sleep?" She moved to sit on the top step in front of him, letting the sun turn her hair a bright copper.

"Good morning, I slept well." They both sipped in silence.

"Well, I go in to work today, so you'll be on your own, unless you want to ride Bandit into town..."

"I think I'll get organized here, but I'd like to ride just around here...is that ok?"

"Well, yes, but remember, you're alone out here, Cliff is about a mile away, so, I want you to be careful. I know you ride well, but there are certain spots where a misstep could injure...you and Bandit."

"Of course, I'll be very careful." He hesitated before answering.

"You promise?"

"I promise." He stood up.

"Ok then, but if you have any problem, or need something...ride down to Cliff's, meet his wife and kids, they'd love to meet you!" She nodded.

"I will do that. And...can I...do you have a library of some kind? I really haven't seen any books." Luke laughed.

"You haven't had a proper tour of the house! Look in the back room, end of the hall. There are some boxes of stuff in there, I'm sure my books are in there. So, you like to read too?"

"Yes, I do. Maybe there's a library in town I can visit?"

"I think there's a cache of books connected to the church...First Congregational and Parsonage. It's near City Hall. I can check on that for you today."

"If you have time, thank you."

"I'll make time."

He headed toward the barn to saddle up Charlotte. He greeted Bandit, rubbing his head over the stall gate and whispered,

"You take good care of Tabitha today, ya hear?" Bandit snorted and pressed his velvety nose into his gloved hand.

Luke swung into the saddle, and waved at Tabitha, still on the porch.

"I'll be back before dark, and make a list of anything you might need, or want, ok?"

"Ok...be careful!"

She stood and waved at him, and he started down the drive at a slow lope. He stopped at Cliff's on the way, seeing him in his front field. He dismounted and they shook hands.

"Luke, how's it going over at your place?" Cliff wore a white hat and was clearing some rocks into a wheelbarrow. His teenage son was working nearby loosening more rocks with a hoe in a chopping fashion. He stopped his work and came over to the men.

"Heh, pretty not too bad!" Luke answered, shaking Jeremy's hand.

"Just wanted to let you know Tabitha is staying at home alone, today. I told her to come over and say heh."

"Good 'nuf! She can meet Martha and the girls. I'm sorry I didn't get to meet her when you brought her back. Jeremy could check on her sometime today if y'all want."

"Mighty nice of you, thanks Jeremy! Ok, better get."

Luke rode away, feeling a little better.

Cowboy gear, c. 1890

Luke stayed busy until 3:00 that afternoon. He made his stops, talked with town members, checked on supplies, and took Johnson out for a noon meal. It was a daily balancing act to check on needs in the town and outlier areas. Luke knew just about everyone as a result of constantly moving around the area during his regular days to keep in touch with the locals. He suddenly remembered his promise to Tabitha to check on the library. He thought it a good idea to check now before it got too late, and then make his way home.

He cantered down Gurley Street, the main street in town, and searched for the church across the street and north to ride up to the plain clapboard building of First

Congressional and Parsonage Church. It was set on an acre of grassland, with two buildings. A sign had been erected in front of the door stating its name.

He tied off his horse and knocked on the wooden double-door entry. He didn't get any response, and walked around the side to the back. There he found a horse and wagon tied up, with feed and water under an awning, and he noticed the back door was ajar.

Stepping up, he knocked loudly on the door, and called out as he slowly opened the door into the inside.

"Hello, anyone here?"

He stepped in, letting his eyes get used to the darker inside.

"Sheriff Richmond here. Anybody here?"

He walked through an ancillary room, noting boxes stacked against both walls. Crossing over the threshold into the Nave and Chancel, it was deserted. He stepped into the Narthex, and a small side room, probably where the Pastor had an office but still no owner of the horse and wagon.

He walked back toward where he entered, and walking around the other side, he noticed the long, low building, and the entry door was open. He entered calling out again.

"Hello? Anyone here?"

"Yes?" A woman's voice loudly responded, and there she sat, behind a wooden desk, in front of a blackboard and chairs and tables stored to her right.

Luke found himself looking into a familiar face, and took off his hat. Renee looked carefully at him, studying his face and clear, blue eyes. The door was open behind him with sunshine streaming in, so she had to stare a bit before she recognized the handsome face. He smiled appreciatively at her, noting that she was even more beautiful than he remembered from their run-in at the Mercantile.

Her dark eyes underneath her bright blonde hair warmed up and her smile grew as she recognized him. He cleared his throat.

"Well, hello again, Miss…" he let his voice trail off. Renee cleared her throat too.

"Hello again to you, sir!" She noticed his badge. "Do you work for the Sheriff?"

"I uh, am the Sheriff. I'm Luke, Luke Richmond." She stood and slowly walked to stand in front of him. She outstretched her right hand.

"I'm Renee Boudreau, and I'm the teacher here!"

"Very nice to meet you . . . again!"

They pumped hands, and Renee released hers first, and folded them behind her. She felt herself blushing.

"So, "she said. "We bumped into each other two times yesterday and here you are! What can I do for you?"

He held his hat in both hands, and asked,

"Well, I understand you may have a library here?"

She rolled her eyes.

"If you want to call it that...yes, I am building a collection I started long ago. I have about a hundred books so far, but need so many more! They are books I've been able to get, some donated, most from my personal collection and many purchased. I wish I had a thousand, but, well...teachers don't make a lot of money, and I don't receive much of an allowance from the State! "

"Well, I have a collection too of my own, say...what if we went through what I have and see if we might add it to yours?" Renee's smile widened.

"My goodness! Well, I say...thank you very much, and I will go through them myself...if you're sure...I mean, that's very generous of you...Sheriff."

"Please, call me Luke. I've read almost all of them so you're welcome to them. I still have most of them boxed up at home."

"Oh, how wonderful!" She clasped her hands together in excitement.

"Good enough, and say, I wonder if I might borrow some from your collection?"

"Of course! Many of them are for elementary school children, of course, but there are also some novels, dictionaries, atlas, and some reference books too. Was this for...personal use?"

"No, my daughter has come to stay with me for a while, from back east. I'm sure she had access to a nice library in Philadelphia and New York, and she asked me to check on our library here. I wasn't even sure you had one."

"Well, right now, I'll say it's starting to shape up already!"

She asked carefully,

"How old is she...your daughter?"

"She's sixteen. She's been living with her mother. We...were married, but we aren't any more."

They let silence pass between them for a moment.

Then, "Well, it's nice to meet Prescott's teacher, aren't you done for the year?" He looked around.

"Yes, as you might tell, it's clean up and reorganize time now!"

"Apparently! Well...why don't I arrange to get a wagon and I can bring the boxes here, whenever you say."

"I have a wagon, maybe I can...pick them up...tomorrow morning?"

"We can ride over and take your wagon out to my place, just outside of town. I can tie up Charlotte to the back. Those boxes will be heavy. I would feel better taking you out to the ranch myself, I wouldn't want you to get lost!"

She beamed, clapping her hands together again. "Excellent! Oh, Sheriff...I mean, Luke, you have brightened this already bright day!"

Luke looked down. "And you mine."

He said this low and soft. They were caught up in a long gaze together. Renee felt herself blushing again.

"Well, I guess I'll let you get back to work. What would be a good time tomorrow?"

"Oh, early! I'm here by 7:00 am, so any time after that."

"That works for me, ok then, see you in the mornin'!"

"Fine." She started to walk him out, and he felt a twinge of excitement as they walked side-by-side. The wind ruffled his hair and he put his hat on. They walked to where his horse was tied.

"Oh my!" Renee exclaimed upon seeing his brown and white Appaloosa. "She's beautiful, Luke! Where did you find her?"

Luke laughed. Charlotte snorted and backed up, moving alongside her master, eyes on the strange woman standing near him. He steadied her, and held the reins tightly toward himself, lest she get spooked.

"Well, she sort of found me. It's a good story, I'll tell you some other time."

"On the way to your ranch tomorrow!" She decided...

"Well...Renee...off I go." He put out his hand. "It was a pleasure to meet you."

She took his hand, this time lightly, this time just holding it. She gently squeezed it, and softly said,

"My pleasure too..." There was something that moved her upon meeting his eyes, being so close to him, hearing him breathe...something beneath her heart, something she'd never felt before. She had no words for the feeling, but it left her feeling a little confused, or was she just dizzy? He stepped back, and swung up onto Charlotte. She stepped lively, prancing a bit in place. She moved athletically, smoothly, easily. How fast she must run, Renee thought.

And with that, Luke turned her toward the west, and began his trek home. He waved at her goodbye, as she did him. Without any prodding or even a squeeze of his heels, Charlotte took off like a shot to take her master home. Renee looked after them until they disappeared.

Charlotte's Run Home

She poured herself another cup of coffee. Looking around the kitchen, she thought about how much exploring she had to do. She'd never ran a kitchen before, or cooked a meal, or cleaned a house, but she was willing to. She walked slowly around the cabinets, opening doors, seeing what it was stocked with. The ice box had milk and butter inside. She pumped the well water pump on the side of the big porcelain sink and after three pumps up and down water spilled out. She opened the oven. The ceiling was high, and the floor was stone tiles.

There was a door that led outside, and she stepped onto a small back porch. She gazed at all the land around her, flat grass and shrub surrounding the house, and pine trees reached into the blue sky behind. There was a metal silo at the side of the barn, which was long and low, and could hold several horses in stalls.

Some paperbacks, some beautiful bindings, and some very old books were among the treasure troves she found. Box after box revealed new and exciting titles she couldn't wait to open. Titles like,

Pride and Prejudice, by Jane Austen.

Jane Eyre, by Charlotte Brontë

Frankenstein, by Mary Wollstonecraft Shelley.

Wuthering Heights, by Emily Brontë

The Picture of Dorian Gray, by Oscar Wilde.

Little Women, by Louise May Alcott

Dracula, by Gram Stoker

Anna Karenina, by Leo Tolstoy

Excitedly, she found Sherlock Holmes, Poems by Emily Dickenson, and Walt Whitman novels. Her father was quite a reader! She couldn't have been happier with his selections...or...perhaps, these had belonged to her mother, who read as avidly as Tabitha but she'd left without much luggage when she had fled Arizona to return home to Philadelphia.

Of course...it dawned on her.

She went on to find two dictionaries, an atlas, and a few western novels.

Well, these could be her father's. She actually knew very little about him, but deep inside, she believed he was a good man who spoke the truth. And she knew she wanted to know all who he was, after all, she had come almost 3,000 miles to be here. She felt safe and taken care of and any fear had fallen away from her.

She smiled as she carried about twenty books and lay them on the desk in her room. The desk was bare, and she imagined he had acquired it only for her visit. She reorganized her plain armoire, and put the clothes she wanted to freshen in a pile. She explored the parlor, and decided to do some dusting and straightening up.

She peeked inside the kitchen cupboards again and knew she'd have to get a cookbook to know how to put together ingredients for bread, soup, and stew. There was so much about life in this foreign environment that she knew nothing about. Since she thrived on learning new things, she knew she would do her best to learn how to do the things she'd never done before in her prior life back east.

She took a glass of milk and ate some fruit. She tied her hair in a high ponytail, and she made her way out to the barn. She wore her breeches, boots, and a light shirt tied up around her waist. It was already getting hot.

Bandit whinnied at her approach to his stall, nuzzling his nose into her hand, and the two got reacquainted. Then, she saddled him up, seeing that her father had fed both horses that morning, and off they went on an outdoor adventure. She loved wearing her new hat which provided ample shade from the strengthening sun.

Meanwhile, Luke's trek home was unlike any other time he headed home before. He was leaving a woman who had left her effect upon him in an unprecedented physical way. He felt flushed, short of breath, and there was a fluttering in his belly. Anxious but not nervous; dizzy but not weak. What in the name of God was occurring?

He was also riding towards his own home in a different way. It wasn't standing empty. There was someone waiting for him there. His daughter had come into his fulfilling, yet lonely life. He wanted to hug someone. He wiped his sleeve across his eyes, as his eyes welled up with tears. "Damn!" he yelled to no one, spurring Charlotte to speed up.

Tabitha started down the dirt trail to meet up with their neighbors.

They cantered down the well-known path, which Bandit knew well. One mile took about sixteen minutes as it was flat land, and she turned into the fenced gate, which was open and she slowed to a walk up the front drive. The first people she saw were two little girls running outside and standing on the porch, staring at her. They were both dressed in identical dresses with white aprons, and smiling, calling their mother.

"Mommy! Mommy! She's here!"

They were dark haired and looked so excited it made Tabitha laugh. Could they be waiting just for her? A dark-haired woman wearing a dress and similar white apron joined them, wiping her hands off on a small towel, and she watched as Tabitha rode up and smiled widely, stepping down the steps, followed by her little girls.

"You must be Tabitha! I'm Margaret, Cliff's wife!"

Tabitha walked Bandit up to the tie-up rail, and dismounted.

"Yes, I am! Nice to meet you!"

They shook hands, and the girls gathered on the side of her, acting shy but peeking out to stare at the visitor.

"And who are these pretty girls?"

They both lit up at that, and stood straight up now.

"Yes, this is Mary, and this is Madeline!"

Tabitha looked at each pretty face. They giggled, and retreated again behind their mother. Margaret raised up her skirts and led the way up to the front porch.

"I like your riding outfit! Well, come on in, Tabitha! I have some tea ready!"

The girls ran in ahead of them both, and Tabitha entered their very modest but large front room.

"Let's go into the kitchen!"

Tabitha followed her into the very large kitchen that had a long wooden table set for six people with high-back chairs. There was a bowl of fruit in the center.

"Take a seat, sugar and milk is on the table."

Tabitha took the closest chair, removed her hat and gloves, and put them on the chair beside her. The girls clamored to bring tea cups and saucers, and placed them on the table. The design was simple, not fine China as her mother had, but a metal teapot on the stove with hot water and loose tea in the metal tea ball. She could smell the rich aroma of the black tea, and put a bit of milk into her cup. Margaret poured the two of them a cup, and sat down across from Tabitha, and the girls stood by her side, staring at her.

Tabitha took a sip, as did Margaret. They were quiet for a moment.

"Girls, why don't you get us some cookies, then let us have some time to talk!" They scrambled to get a plate of cookies that had powdered sugar atop them. They placed it on the table between the two women, and Mary asked her mother,

"Can we show Tabitha our room later, Mommy?"

"Yes, please!" Madeline chimed in.

Margaret nodded her head.

"Yes darlings, now go see what your brother's up to!" The girls giggled and ran out the back door. Margaret shook her head, smiling.

"As you can see, we don't have many visitors out here! They were so excited to meet you!"

"And I want to meet you and your family. I don't know anyone out here yet! You're the first!"

"Well, I know we will make friends quickly! How are you feeling, being out here for the first time, far from your home?"

Tabitha breathed deeply. "Well...I'm not sure yet...Luke is welcoming, and the house is comfortable...I love to ride, and want to explore the area. I... don't know how things are out here...I guess I have a lot to learn."

"Well, you seem to be fitting in well...I will help you anyway I can. You just need to ask!"

They sipped tea as they chatted about their lifestyles. Margaret was very kind and open about her background. She'd moved here with Cliff, her husband from Texas. They homesteaded there and raised a small cattle farm. They raised their son, Jeremiah (Jeremy) who was nineteen, and the identical twin girls, Mary and Madeline, who were eight years old. Margaret had a vegetable garden, some chickens, and liked to bake. She offered to write down some recipes for Tabitha, asking what ingredients she already had, and sharing her some pantry items.

She also placed a cookbook in her hand, pointing out she had another.

Tabitha asked her if she had ever met her mother.

"Yes, I did meet Sophia. She was...a beautiful woman, very quiet, but she never came over to visit." Margaret sipped at her tea before continuing.

"I didn't know she was pregnant with you when she left. When Luke shared the news about you, I felt so sorry...for both of you, what you must have felt about it all. I really didn't know her at all.'

"I...didn't really know what to think when she told me about Luke. I had no idea. My step-father, who I thought was my father...well, I love him very much. But when my mother explained her life here and her move back to be with her family, I just knew that I would want to meet him."

"Do you know yet how long you will stay? Are you still in school?"

"No, I finished Upper School. I suppose I'll attend college at some point ...don't really know for certain what I will do...I don't know how long I will stay. But...I like the space out here...I never liked the city very much. It was all too busy. And... I never wore breeches before in my life!"

Both ladies laughed out loud.

It was a funny moment.

Maybe she was fitting in!

The girls came back with a tall, slim boy, pulling him into the kitchen. He was dressed in pants and shirt and soil-covered work boots. His dark hair fell over his eyes, and he looked irritated about having to make an appearance.

Margaret said,

"Jeremy, this is our neighbor, Tabitha. Please say hello!" Jeremy pushed his hair back from his forehead and shook off his sisters holding onto each hand. He focused on her, and at first looked surprised, then shuffled over to her, and extended his right hand.

"Hello, nice ta meet ya."

Tabitha pumped his hand, and gave him a nice smile since he looked so uncomfortable. He then smiled too.

"Welcome ta Prescott!"

"Thank you, nice to meet you too!"

He held her hand still, and looked more relaxed.

"So...where are ya from?"

"Philadelphia."

"Do ya like it here?"

"Yes, I do!"

The girls clamored in between them squealing,

"Come to our room! Now, Tabitha!"

They pulled at her hands and she giggled.

"Ok!"

They each held a hand and led her upstairs, and into their bedroom that they shared.

She oohed and aahed at the toys they presented to her that they had. They ended up jumping on their little beds on opposite sides of the room and asking her questions as she sat on the rug between them.

"How old are you? What do you like to do? Can we come see your room?"

"Um...sixteen, ride horses and read, and yes!"

After a bit, they all three went downstairs and met up with Margaret. Jeremy had returned to the fields.

Tabitha carried a paper bag with her new cookbook, yeast, sugar and some other ingredients for dinner out to Bandit, who had been given water. Tabitha reminded herself that she needed to keep him watered with this warmer weather more.

Margaret hugged her closely, and told her how delightful it was to spend the afternoon with her. The girls both hugged her at the same time.

"Come back soon!" they yelled together.

Tabitha thanked them all, and swung up the Bandit's back to make the short drive back, but as she turned to start down the drive, she noticed Jerimiah standing straight and staring at her, waving his arm her way. She waved back.

She had met her first four friends. She smiled widely as she led Bandit home. She was fitting in!

Tabitha and Bandit

When Bandit arrived at their ranch, Tabitha led him along the perimeter of the property. They stepped carefully, following her father's instructions, and they safely made it all the way around. She came up on a quail family, a mother and four chicks trotting on the ground, running away from her quickly and disappearing into some brush. She longed to explore into the pines, but would wait until she could do so with her father. She had walked Toby around the property a bit, and wondered how he would fare running alongside her when she rode Bandit.

Upon returning home, she rubbed down her steed and rolled up her sleeves.

Tabitha got started on a first-time adventure...kneading dough for a loaf of bread. She put a pot of water on the stove and prepared a stew with ingredients Margaret had given her; chicken breast, vegetables from her garden, and makings for a broth. She set the dining room table with cloth napkins she found in a drawer and silverware, plates and salt and pepper shakers she'd filled. She went out front and snipped some wild flowers, and put them in a glass for a centerpiece.

She wore a towel around her waist to do as an apron, looking forward to making something palatable for them both.

She'd changed into a very simple skirt and blouse with a belt cinching her narrow waist. She put the raised bread into the gas oven to bake.

They both went out on the porch to watch the sun set and wait for her father to arrive home. She leaned against a rail post, and sighed into the evening. She'd had a busy day, and liked meeting the neighbors. She scratched Toby's head and neck as they looked out to the dirt road eastward to watch for Charlotte cantering home.

Margaret had asked how she'd felt about all this newness happening around her and inside of her, but

Tabitha knew her father deserved some consideration on how he was feeling as well.

Did he really enjoy having his unknown daughter plunked down into his life whom he knew nothing about? What if he had been used to...having...company...overnight in his home, and now...he didn't think he should? Was he...happy? She was mature enough to understand the relationship between a man and a woman and what that entailed. She'd received information from schoolmates and had endured an awkward few words from her mother about the sexual side of life. Her father was confident, attractive and must meet people all day long, would she hold him back?

Then she sat up straight...there was a stir of dust far down the road, and faint hoof sounds in the silent air, and she stood as Toby already had perked-up ears in that direction, curious about who approached their sanctuary. She then saw Charlotte loping, and a black-hatted man egging her on as if in a hurry to arrive back home, and as he rounded the fencing and turned towards her, she could see the smiling relief in his face that she was alive and well and awaiting his return. Toby started barking, standing guard right in front of her.

Luke dismounted and, hesitating a second, strode to meet her where she stood. They eyed each other, and then slowly she allowed him to enfold her in his hug. They held each other for about half a minute, then he held her away from him to look into her eyes.

"So glad to see you!" She was smiling too.

"So glad to see you!"

She walked him to the barn as he started to tell her about his day. It felt to her as if they'd done this before, many an evening. It felt natural, and so pleasant.

Father and Daughter

With her coffee on the porch step, Tabitha found herself waiting once again for the return of her father the next day. Dinner had been tasty the night before, but she wanted to hone her cooking skills and would ask Margaret for more advice, as well as pore over her cookbook. Her father had left over an hour ago to town to pick up Miss Boudreau and her wagon, and the plan was for her to pick up the boxes of books that Tabitha had found in the spare room, minus the few she held for herself. Then, they would both accompany her back to the school to help set them up, and tie up Bandit to the back, and since Charlotte was at the tie up at the school from his morning ride, he could go to work from there for the rest of the day and Tabitha could ride Bandit back.

They should be over half-way home by now. Tabitha wondered for a while why Luke didn't just tell the teacher how to make her way to the ranch, but she'd had a feeling, perhaps in the way his voice slightly lowered when talking about Renee, that he was finding her enjoyable to be with.

Tabitha tried to remember her face and stature from their one-time meeting at the store, but she only could remember short blonde hair and the smart outfit she wore...and her voice; it was strong and confident. As far as she knew, there was no woman in her father's life. Perhaps the two would become more than friends? Her mind went to Jeremy, the first young man she'd met so far. When would it be her time to be coupled up with someone? Did she even want to be? She'd never had a boyfriend before, only one girlfriend, Delia, who went to her private school back home.

She stood and stretched, and turned inside to pour another cup of coffee. She and her father liked it strong and black. The boxes had been carried downstairs and were stacked on the floor near the door, ready to be taken and enjoyed by future students.

Toby made a yelp from the porch, signaling someone nearing the house. Tabitha put down her coffee and came outside to see a pretty draft horse pulling a small wagon with a very attractive couple sitting in the leather bench seat in front. Tabitha waved widely as they came up the drive, and Toby stood dutifully by her side, but was shaking in anticipation and wanted to run out and greet the two. Both had wide smiles on their faces, and Tabitha smoothed her long hair up in a ponytail. She wanted to look presentable after working all morning cleaning and exploring inside, which she was doing one day at a time.

"Hello-Hello!" Renee called out to the two on the porch, and she held onto her seat until Luke stopped the wagon, then jumped down and ran up to Tabitha, surprising her with a big hug.

"Oh, so good to meet you, Tabitha! Luke has told me so much about you!" Her eyes shone in the sunlight, and her hair looked like gold, curling and bobbing at the ends. She lost her hat in the process, and laughed, dusting it off and planting it back on her head. It was light tan and western style.

"Well, it's good to meet you too, Miss Boudreau! How was the drive over?"

Luke tied up Nicco, Renee's horse, giving his neck a scratch, and answered,

"It was pretty smooth! Guess I don't need to introduce you two!"

"And you can call me Renee, Tabitha, no Miss!"

Tabitha bobbed her head up and down.

"I made fresh coffee if you'd like, and the books are right inside the door!"

She led the way and Renee followed her inside. Luke unhitched the buckboard wagon from Nicco's reins and side straps to water him and rub him down.

"So...I think you're going to be pleased with the titles...Renee. I think these must have belonged to my mother! We...both love to read. Do you have a need for the classics?"

Renee's eyes widened as she opened the first box and gasped.

"Oh my, this is grand!"

She acted as Tabitha had, as if she was opening a treasure chest, handling one book at a time, eyes dancing with anticipation. They both sat cross legged on the floor.

"This is wonderful! I thank you and Luke so much!" She looked directly at Tabitha. "I consider this only a loan, but I hope to replace them all, sometime not too far away."

"I think my father wanted to make a gift of them! I also pulled a few but will give them to you when I'm finished."

"I found a bookshelf I can store them on, but I really need to organize them first, and by the looks of it, I'll need to locate another shelf unit...maybe two!" Tabitha felt joy just watching Renee like a young girl opening up her Christmas presents. She wondered just how young she was.

"Would you like...I mean, can I help? I can certainly arrange them alphabetically...by title or author, or maybe by subject or level of difficulty?"

Renee stared at her wide-eyed.

"Oh my! What an offer! Are you sure? It will take some time, but yes! Yes, of course you can help!"

"I had planned to come with you back to the school today, I can certainly get started!" Renee clapped her hands together.

"Oh, my yes! I can make us some lunch!"

Tabitha felt she had found yet another friend, and only in the first week of her arrival. Renee appeared to be like a girlfriend with her mannerisms and enthusiasm. The two liked each other on the spot and they were to spend many good times together in their futures.

Luke entered and looked down at the two on the floor. He had to laugh.

"You two look like you're having fun!"

Renee stood up in one smooth move and hugged Luke gently.

"This is a wonderful collection, thank you, Luke."

The two exchanged a very happy look, which answered a question for Tabitha...yes, they would become closer than friends.

Sophia Martin

About two weeks after her daughter had left to travel to the other side of the country, Sophia received her first letter, rushing to the parlor to open it and read it alone.

Dear Mother,

I sent this after my first few days so you would be assured that I arrived safely and soundly. The train trip was long but comfortable enough. Thank you for all the "chaperones" you set up for the different stations to watch over me. They were very helpful with answering my several questions as you know I always have!

It is so different out here in the "Wild West." It is quite warm already, dry, with great open land. I am riding daily with Luke. My horse is named Bandit, and is very gentle and careful with me. My father has been very kind and welcoming to me. We do many things. I think he has a lovely ranch house and barn. I think he wants to buy more horses. He works long hours but seems to like what he does.

I have met some nice ladies who live here, a neighbor and the town school teacher, and they have answered my many questions and made me feel welcome.

I miss you and Randolph.

We loaned some books that I found in storage to the teacher for her students to read. Are those yours? Jane Austen and Walt Whitman, I know are two of your favorite authors, so I guess they belong to you when you lived here. I'm sure she will take good care of them, and if you want them shipped back to you, I will let Luke know.

    I am very happy and comfortable here, and agree with you and Randolph that it was a very good idea for me to come here and meet my father. We have a lot in common I am finding. Thank you for making it happen. I don't know how long I will be staying; did you have an idea of what you wish?
    I miss you both very much, and look forward to your letter.
    Love, Tabitha

She read it twice over, and then held it to her chest. The news couldn't have been better. She was thankful to Luke for reacting so well to her sudden, unexpected visit. She didn't leave the man himself. She left the lifestyle. The west was no place for her, and she didn't consider herself spoiled. She was just used to her life the way it had begun...in a large beautiful home, someone else to do the cooking and cleaning which she detested, and stores with couture fashion.

When she had run into women who wore shirts and breeches and rode a horse like a man, she knew she had made a mistake. She'd spent almost all of her time inside the ranch house; she had never ridden atop a horse before and had never wanted to. She'd only sat in Luke's wagon, an uncomfortable and jostling ride, but the only way to reach downtown to see it and shop for things. Her environment had changed from excess to not enough. She surveyed her new life in this rough environment with its dirt sidewalks and roads. There was nothing to do, really, except all the things she detested. The townspeople were backward, awkward, and seemed content living their simple lives. It rarely rained, and everything seemed brown except for the pine trees, which shed messy needles everywhere. The air made her skin feel dry, and she was constantly moisturizing.

However, the winters– they were truly beautiful. The air at the high altitude smelled uniquely fresh, the snow fell for two months, but never reached over two feet in depth, and the valleys filled quickly in spring with green grasses, the varieties she'd never seen before.

She remembered the Mercantile downtown was to be laughed at. It had the merest of supplies, horribly-styled dresses, and shoes and boots that were ugly and unsophisticated. The hats ladies wore were ugly. The food served in restaurants was unpalatable. Vendors had never heard of Champagne. There were some wines, and she loved a good Claret wine, which came from northern California, but it took too long to be shipped over. It seemed everything moved slower and took longer than she was used to. No one seemed to read, there was no newspaper but for the Phoenix Republic, which could take up to four days to get, and to import one in from the east would take over a week. By then it held only old news.

There was actually nothing redeeming about the west, in her opinion. She realized within only a few weeks that the move and the marriage had been just her ploy to move away from her parents who were demanding and controlling.

When she realized she was pregnant, she knew it was a clear sign for her to move back home, back to civilization. She would never have allowed her daughter to be raised in such a desolate environment, and that was why she made the decision to leave. Her mother warned her that she could not tell her husband before she left. He might try to change her mind, or worse, keep her there by force. That would mean a man would try to control her, and her mother wanted that to remain her job. She had to weigh the situation carefully after she'd seen the only doctor near her to tell him her symptoms. Her breasts were tender, her period had ceased, and she was sick every morning. She was tired all of a sudden, but after the doctor's assurance that she was indeed with child, she was surprisingly filled with joy.

She remembered looking in the mirror several times a day to notice any changes, or if she appeared to look any different. She searched for changes in her. She would smile as she spent each day thinking about the impending date of her baby's birth.

She had to send and receive telegrams back and forth to her mother to set up everything carefully. Her mother was able to wire her money for a ticket on the train. Before she started showing she knew she had to leave. She had to set up travel to Yuma in order to meet the train at the station. She wasn't afraid at all to take the trip eastward on her own, the first time she'd ever traveled on her own in her life. She carried a precious gift and had to put her first...and she knew she would be a girl, and she would never control her daughter like her mother had tried to control her. She would raise her to be herself, no matter what.

Looking in the only mirror in their house, she had never looked more beautiful. She placed both of her delicate hands on her abdomen. She sighed at herself and closed her eyes. She was just extremely selfish. She had fallen for a cowboy, and now she realized it was one giant mistake. She couldn't reverse time, so she chose to pretend; she would merely deny and avoid her situation. Once home again she would be fine and pretend all of this never happened.

Her baby was born with her mother by her side. Tabitha was beautiful with a shock of red hair the moment Sophia gave birth. She screamed loudly upon her arrival.

Sophia's mother insisted on holding her daughter's hand during her giving birth at only the very best hospital in Philadelphia. She had the baby's name all picked out...after her mother's name, Tallulah. Sophia hated it. She felt grateful she was named after the President's daughter's name, Sophia Buchanan. She conceded, and then changed it to Tabitha after marrying Randolph Martin two years later, after an enterprising woman who invented the circular saw in the early 1800's. Sophia couldn't do what she'd dreamed of, be an independent entrepreneur, but her daughter could be. And she intended to give her every chance to break into the world of men.

Now looking in the beautiful gilded-edged mirror in her parlor, Sophia was still very attractive, strong, and had a bright mind. Perhaps she could still realize her dreams...perhaps by returning to the very place she loathed to live. Now that her daughter was situated in a growing new territory, she might follow suit. Her daughter sounded happy. That was all that mattered to her. And as her mother, she would do anything to provide for her. She also knew that Tabitha had the same free spirit inside of her that she had. It had only grown stronger inside of her.

She went to the fireplace mantle, and picked up the photo of Tabitha someone had taken when she was eight-years-old in the backyard grounds of the mansion. She looked at her daughter's image, wearing a little red sundress and her hair fell in two long braids. She had on a sweet, innocent smile. Then, Sophia went over to the secretary and sat down, starting to make a list…

Tabitha Martin c. 1880

At dawn, three Navajo men rode their paint horses into the outskirts of the town of Prescott, using deer trails and foraging through wild brush to reach the ranch just east of Lonesome Valley. It was an early morning ascent which started in the Chino Valley area and continued to the "mile high area" of Prescott at the base of Mingus Mountain. They'd ridden hard and fast from the northernmost boundary line of Arizona, almost into Utah. They'd crossed over 300 miles in a few days, faster than any train could cover down the White Man railroad tracks. They hadn't stopped to rest overnight and took care to avoid any White Men. Apache scouts were no doubt positioned high in the hills on watch to protect their tribal communities.

The Apache people were a threatened tribe, and they were a proud and aggressive group of survivors. They would die rather than give up their land, but they were divided into numerous tribal settlements after banding together for over 100 years before. They would rather kill than be killed. Their language was very different from other numerous tribes. It was almost like a secret code they cherished and protected. They had no allies; no other Natives, nor Mexicans, nor White Men. They were desperate, and that is why there were bloody sieges reported and terrorizing accounts of their brutality, but in actuality, they were only defending their place on the earth.

It all was truly confusing, jarring and unbalanced, but it was happening, as if an avalanche, an earthquake, a tidal wave that no human being could arrest. It was unstoppable, these changes and forced adaptations that needed to be made by those who were already in place in the west of this still-new country, being created almost day- by-day.

Aditsan was flanked by Wingo and Tanco. They rode expertly, becoming part of their animals beneath them, dressed in buckskin leather, some beads and feathers, with bow and arrow pouches across their saddle backs. Each had a knife tucked into the side of their breeches. Aditsan also had a revolver, given to him by the friend he came all this way to meet up with again after almost one year had passed.

Luke Richmond was his friend, his spirit brother, and he had given him his best young marc at their first meeting during an ambush, led by a White Man gang. Sheriff Luke had been tracking two thieves with a deputy.

Aditsan remembered that violent and frightening night well, and had told the story many times to others in his tribe. It never failed that they were always perplexed at the tale of a White Man's kindness for a fellow man, no matter him being Indian. It always made him smile, as he was now . . .

Navajo "Wolves," c. 1875

Luke and Renee set off in the wagon on a sunny, warm Tuesday towards his ranch. He pointed out landmarks so that she would know the way on her own. They sat in silence for a ways, and then she asked,

"Tell me about Charlotte."

Luke didn't smile when he readied to tell her the story, a story he'd never told another living soul. It was a tense time ten years prior between the Apaches and the Whites, as well as the Navajo.

He slowed down the rig a bit. And looked straight ahead as he told his story.

"It was a hot summer last year. I had been in Cottonwood to talk with another rancher about his horse stock. It wasn't necessary for me to return to Prescott that day, but I wanted to get back, even though it would be a dark four-hour ride.

"Halfway home, at Lake Wilson I went down the bank to water my horse. I dismounted leading him to the lake, and noticed a campfire on the western edge. It was nice and quiet and I would be glad to hit the sleep roll. I saw flashes of people, Native men, maybe four or five. As I kept watching, suddenly there were cries and horses riding into their camp. My eyes were able to see more clearly in the dark, and as the campers were surprised, one of them was down on the ground.

"I didn't know how many, what tribe, if they were White Men, but I couldn't leave. I stayed on the ground, and checked my gun. It was loaded, and I went to my saddlebag and added loose bullets to my pocket.

"I didn't want to draw attention to myself by riding over to the camp, so I hiked back to the road, and came around staying hidden in the tree line. I heard more yelling, and as I got closer, I could recognize the dress and colors belonging to the Apache tribe of several braves. There had been several skirmishes in the past decade, even though as a whole they had tapered off with time. The other tribe was either Yavapai or Navajo.

"I was close enough to shoot, and as one Apache was wielding a hatchet over the head of the other, who was without a weapon and using his foot to push his foe in the chest to knock him down, he fell back and the attacker now had the advantage. I... had to act fast. I shot twice. He fell. All eyes were now looking my way. I never knew if the Apache saw me, but the silence was eerie, as they got to their horses and rode away. They could have carried guns themselves, but maybe they thought there was an Indian Posse coming down on them. I don't know...everything happened so quickly.

"I stayed where I was until I could no longer hear them ride out. By the fire, I could see there were three Indians standing. The one on the ground slowly rose, staring into the trees to see me. I stood up, and he motioned me over to them. I walked the 20 or so feet, and the three gathered together, standing as still as a rock. I lifted my gun over my head to show I wasn't going to shoot. I said,

"I'm Luke."

"The one in the fight with the one I shot put up his hand to me, and walked up and said he was Aditsan of the Navajo Nation." He spoke English.

"He asked where my horse was, and sent one of his men to go fetch it. He invited me to camp with them. They dragged the dead Apache and the dead member of their tribe away, laying their man across his mount, leaving the Apache in the dark

"The next day, Aditsan and I got to know each other. They ended up coming to my ranch on their way south, and I gave them one of my rifles and rounds; I also gave Aditsan a revolver. When they left, he thanked me for his life.

"He became my friend. I...had never killed anyone in my life. That was a first for me. I hope to never have to again."

Renee had listened patiently to his story and shook her head, putting her hand on his hands holding the reins. He stopped the wagon.

"Luke, that was so brave, and must have been frightening for you."

"Honestly it was."

"He was lucky you were there. So, was he the one who gave you Charlotte?"

Luke nodded his head.

"On his trip up north later that month, he rode to the ranch alone, leading the most beautiful horse I'd ever seen.

Charlotte was barely a full grown mare, and a purebred Appaloosa."

He added with obvious appreciation,

"She was one of the horses he'd been trading for. He gave her to me, just like that. She was on a rope, and I tried to give him a halter and reins for his horse but he refused.

"We ate and he went on his way. His English wasn't great and he was always real quiet, speaking only if he needed to, but this visit, he talked more. I guess he felt more comfortable with me. I thanked him, but he thanked me. Off he went.

"That's why she's so important to you...you treat her with such...honor."

"I'm honored to call her mine."

"Why the name Charlotte?"

Luke laughed.

"My mother's name!"

They laughed together, and rode in silence once again...until Luke said,

"Your turn."

"My turn?"

"To tell a story."

Her face grew dark, and Luke pulled up the reins again. "My...parents...they were killed in an Apache raid. We lived in St. Johns, where my mother taught Apache children at the mission church. My brother Paul and I were just kids. It was in the middle of the night, without warning. They came in, and as we stayed hidden..."

She faltered, and held her hands tightly together in her lap. It took a moment for her to continue.

"They axed my father first, then...my mother. We hid in a cellar that was entered into through their bedroom, hidden under a rug. It was kept for storage, but we used it to hide.

"We heard stomping and slamming around above us, and waited until we heard silence to come out. They had stolen several things. We sat shaking for what seemed hours, and I cried, but Paul just held me and said it would be all right. Never had I felt so vulnerable."

She shook her head.

"My brother was only four years older than me...we were both children basically. We had horses, chickens, goats and a milk cow, but they took the horses.

"He covered our parents with bedding, and got us over to our neighbors, taking only a few possessions. Bless them, they let us live with them...the McCallans...they were older and had no children.

"During the next four years. I couldn't go back to the house, but after a time, Paul went back with a wagon and got what he thought I would want. He buried Mom and Dad in the back. He packed and brought me some of our parents' things, our clothes, and eventually all the animals.

"When Paul turned eighteen, he brought us here because of his job on the Anguses' Ranch."

Luke watched her emotional retelling of her story. She didn't cry, but even with years in the passing, he knew it hurt her heart to remember such a violent night. She shook her head and weakly smiled, looking at him.

"It never gets easier to remember, and through all of it, I am so grateful for Paul. I don't know what would have happened to me if not for him. We had one rifle, and my father didn't have a chance to even use it. They took that too, of course."

"Are you sure they were Apache?"

"No, but those at the church told us they must have been, since there had been a rash of attacks in the area recently that were known to be from Apache tribes."

"I'd...like to talk about what happened more with you, and what experience I have had with them, but...for now, I think we should get you and Tabitha together with those books before much longer...what do ya say?"

She looked at him slyly.

"There is one really big regret I will always have. My parents moved here from France, and my mother would tell me stories about all the beautiful garments made in Paris that she dreamed of wearing. Especially the hats and scarves . . . she was going to own both and wear them some day!"

"Well, maybe you'll have to wear them for her instead!"

They eyed each other as if they had, quite remarkably, been friends for much longer than one week. Then Luke shook the reins and they continued to the ranch, talking about her teaching and some parts of his job. She was soon smiling again, and he was grateful. He understood the darkness in death, especially of a loved one. But as such a young child, he imagined it was much, much harder to understand. He shared about how lovely Tabitha's visit had been and left the details for another time. Renee hadn't asked about her sudden visit to see her father, which he appreciated. Silence was enjoyable too with Renee. He was growing very fond of her company, and hoped their time together didn't end with this trip.

When they rounded the posts that led up his drive and he spied his daughter on the porch, he was filled with hope...and love.

Renee and Tabitha

Renee and Tabitha sat among the boxes in the back of the wagon, and Luke drove them to town to unload the books at the school. They chatted the whole way there, about school, Philadelphia, and Prescott. The two ladies found it was easy to talk to each other, and Luke was silent, letting them chitter-chatter. He enjoyed listening. He wasn't used to being around women in general, let alone his daughter and his new friend who happened to be a very attractive and interesting woman.

They passed tall pines, cactus and scrub oak. There wasn't a wind, and the air was pleasant. As Luke looked at the sky, it was cloudless and ice blue. He felt a certain comfort in the moment that he hadn't felt since coming to the area yet. It was a sense of peace, being in the right place at the right time.

Since meeting Renee and holding her in a hug, he was also experiencing a newfound feeling...that of awe and caring. When he was near her, even as now, not even touching, the earth sometimes disappeared underneath his feet. He was on new footing. He toggled between excitement, and some fear. He was 35 years old, and she was 26, and they came from different worlds, but everything she said was filled with either joy or a highly-perceptive response, which he appreciated in a person.

His thoughts left him with a smile, and up ahead was the bend that led to town where he would find Charlotte awaiting him to take him back to work. He was reconsidering returning to town...

He parked the rig and went straight over to the step-down bumper to help first his daughter, then Renee off the back end of the wagon. They were still chatting.

"Tabitha, come on in and look around? Maybe you have some ideas of where to put things!" The two women left to go inside the classroom. Luke went over to Charlotte, who was under the lean-to, and she whinnied softly at his return. He stroked her head and pressed his cheek to her for a moment.

"You are such a gift to me."

He pictured Aditsan's dark-brown face, dark eyes, and long black hair. The memories had flooded back to him after telling Renee about the incident that happened not so long ago.

He reined up Bandit, and unharnessed Nicco. Charlotte whinnied, prancing in place. Rubbing all three down, he guided all three to shelter under the lean-to. He thought he could easily lengthen the awning to make more shade. He had become quite a carpenter since having to use a hammer and a nail often to make repairs in the beginning on his current house, and later to build the barn. He saddled Charlotte and walked her over to the classroom, tying her up to the wagon. The door was open to the inside, and Luke stuck his head in.

"Heh, ladies?" They both stopped chatting. "I'm going to bring the boxes in, then head out. Both came over to him and nodded.

"Luke, we can certainly help!"

The three of them made easy work of unloading the wagon.

"Tabitha has some ideas about rearranging the classroom!" Renee said.

Luke smiled widely at her.

"She's already made improvements to the house!"

Luke looked at Tabitha.

"You gonna be able to find your way home ok?" She nodded.

"Yes, I know the landmarks!"

She came over to him and hugged him.

"Thanks for letting me come!"

She turned and started opening boxes. Renee stood, and gazed at Luke.

"Well...I'll...walk you out, then!"

Renee crossed the floor, and walked Luke out to the wagon to untie Charlotte.

"Did I tell you how much I appreciate your kindness?" She asked him, standing close.

"Did I tell you I appreciate your friendship, to me and my daughter?"

Luke looked down at her pretty face. She had a smudge on her cheek, and he raised up his hand to wipe it away. She caught his hand. He took her hand in his, and kissed the back of it. They stood quietly, so close, and he wanted to kiss her but didn't dare, not yet. He wondered if she did too.

Renee didn't feel embarrassed, only butterflies in her stomach and a dryness of her throat surprised her, and she moved to hug him. He held her as long as she stayed in his embrace.

"Would you like to come to dinner sometime soon? Tabitha is becoming a good cook." Renee backed up a step.

"Yes, I would love to! Name the day." Luke smiled.

"How about Friday night, say 6 o'clock?"

"I look forward to it!"

Luke left the school a little more elated. He actually started whistling on the way to the station. His lips had touched her skin, and he reckoned he would kiss her lips soon enough.

Wild West Lovers

Friday was a busy one for both Renee and Tabitha. As the only teacher at the only school in the Prescott area, Renee felt an obligation to fill several roles besides being the best teacher she could be. It was, after all, her first and only job ever. She put in almost as many hours during weekends as she did when school was in session. Earlier, Tabitha had filled two large shelf units with books that her brother helped her acquire, after painting them white. Today, Renee patiently logged each book's title, author and subject. She would fill out catalog cards for them all and place them in boxes for students to use. She would then affix tags in alphabetical order as to author, and nonfiction in subject categories.

Tabitha was making purchases at the grocery for dinner tonight, for the three of them, and wanted it to be special. She mopped the floors, washed windows, and weeded the surrounding flower beds which surrounded the house. Renee was bringing wine and dessert at her insistence. Tabitha hummed as she prepared a grand meal, as the one found in the cookbook Margaret had given her.

At the Mercantile, she'd looked for a new outfit, but didn't find anything to her taste. The merchant told her the new catalog would be arriving soon for the Summer Issue for ladies dresses and accessories from mail order companies just starting out; these included Montgomery Ward and Sears and Roebuck. She was assured she'd have more choices then.

Tabitha had gratefully uncovered linen napkins and tablecloths that looked like they'd never been used, probably something her mother had probably purchased years before. It was at first odd to touch and handle the things her mother had bought and used. They were all her mother's taste...delicate, expensive, unique.

She was grateful too for the myriad of pots and pans she could use. She'd chosen the recipe for roast chicken, green beans, mashed potatoes and fresh baked bread.

She'd also make gravy from the drippings. Renee was making a pie for their dessert.

She'd so enjoyed their day together spent at school, and the sandwiches and lemonade for lunch. She'd loved school herself, and though she might not have planned her future of academia, she liked the story Renee told her about how she loved learning, and took a certification test for the legal ability to become a teacher. Could that be something she would want to take on? It certainly was something to consider.

She also considered herself an apt and avid horsewoman. Would she rather help her father out with a real horse ranch? She had been schooled in riding, English and Western style, and had ridden some esteemed breeds in her time, starting at the age of five. Her mother had insisted.

She had decided to start a diary of her daily activities, musings, and ideas she had about such things. She chose a plain-paged book with no lines, in a pretty binding of silk with flowers. She'd bought a proper ink pen as well, and note cards and stationery for letters she might send. She also bought a little gift for Renee, to put on her teacher's desk. A pretty silver bell to ring. It was in the shape of an apple, which was a well-known icon for teaching.

While awaiting her bread and chicken to be ready, Tabitha dug into more housework. She shook out the rugs, swept the wooden floors, and wiped down the oil lamps. She cleaned the glass of the China cabinet, polished and covered the dining room table with a lace tablecloth, and made the kitchen counters sparkle. She swept the front porch, and a brand new concept came over her as she put away her cleaning tools. She'd never done the chores for any household before; she was enjoying it.

Luke's day went more slowly and quietly, with not much occurring that was out of the ordinary. He made his stops at businesses and had everyone help clean desks and floors at the station. He tended to paperwork, and decided to reorganize all the files. He hadn't gone through the metal file cabinet that stood in the corner of his office in months. Now was as good of a time as any.

He went over to it, thinking of the evening ahead, and had been thinking about it all day long, his reason trying to keep busy. He didn't know this feeling of joy...he found Renee's face dancing in his head, her voice light and musical, her soft skin. She made him feel almost dizzy.

He laughed aloud, and pulled open the top metal drawer. He would see her in three hours. He would also stop by the Mercantile on the way home.

For his Lady...

He rode up and straight into the barn to stall Charlotte. He heard Bandit whinny, along with another horse. He checked the far stall and noticed Renee's horse with his neck straining over the stall gate to see who had entered. Luke gave Nicco a head scratch.

"Well, hi there, friend! Where's your mistress?"

Nicco snorted and nodded his big head and neck in response. He greeted Bandit, and rubbed down his Appaloosa steed. From his saddle bag, he delicately handled the paper-wrapped flowers and exposed the beautiful blossoms of pink and yellow roses. He quickly checked the water and feed, and strode to the house.

When he entered the house, a delicious aroma wafted through the air, making him smile. He entered through the archway into the dining room, where his daughter was setting the table.

"For your table, ma'am!" He handed the bouquet to her, and she exclaimed.

"Oh, they're beautiful! I'm sure I can find a vase. How was your day?!"

Tabitha was wearing her eastern clothes, a beautiful cotton sleeveless peach-colored dress, over which she wore a white cotton apron. Her hair was done up on her head and she wore earrings and a necklace. She looked beautiful.

"Oh my..." he sighed. "You look lovely."

"Thank you..." she hesitated just a moment, and for the first time, said the word, "...father."

She blushed. He smiled in appreciation.

"I better go get cleaned up and put on a proper shirt, at least! Where's Renee?"

"Oh, she's busy in the kitchen...you go on up, dinner will be ready in a bit!"

He nodded.

"Yes, ma'am!" He retreated, and took the stairs two at a time.

Downstairs, the ladies were putting the finishing touches on dinner. Renee had helped immensely. Her dessert was a lemon meringue pie she'd made at her home. The wine was opened, and she polished three long-stemmed crystal glasses to place by each setting. She'd officiated over the cooking, teaching Tabitha many tricks she'd learned along the way. All was ready, they'd turned off the oven gas, and carefully Renee showed her how to carefully wrap the loaf of bread in cheesecloth, putting it on top of the oven in a basket to cool but not too quickly to deflate the insides.

She also instructed her exactly how to make a gravy from the drippings from the bird, using flour, salt and pepper and the flavored fat at the bottom of the roast pan. Renee remarked on the beauty of the china set, and asked if the set belonged to her mother.

"I would think so! I haven't asked my father yet." Renee raised an eyebrow, not having heard her call Luke "father." It sounded right for her to call him that. She had only called him "my father" in a more formal way. Renee opened up the back door to air out the kitchen, as the sun beat down that afternoon.

"I think I'll pour the wine."

Renee checked her reflection in the mirror for a moment before going to the table.

She had chosen a tightly-cinched emerald-green dress that draped across her chest and arms. She wore crystal earrings and a matching choker necklace, simple but elegant. Low heels of black peeked underneath the floor-length gown. She rarely dressed up, but decided it would be nice to bring the dress in wrapping to change into from her riding gear. Tabitha had told her after she'd changed clothes in her room and came downstairs that she looked like a princess. Her bright blonde hair had a silver clip in the back and standing there now, she hoped Luke would like her look.

"Stunning…" His low strong voice carried over the space between them as he stood looking so handsome in a black cotton shirt and jeans. He was unabashedly staring at her, and she nervously laughed, and stepped over to the table.

"Thank you, Luke. Some wine?"

He stood still, and could only gaze at her. He'd never seen such a beautiful vision in his life. Yes, his wife had been attractive, but this woman who stood in front of him now made him want to shield his eyes. It was as if she was luminous.

He came over and accepted the red wine. They stood a foot apart, and tinkled their glasses together in a toast.

"What should we toast to?" she asked.

"To two of the most beautiful ladies in all of Prescott I'd think is proper."

They sipped their Cabernet Sauvignon together and stood in silence.

Tabitha appeared through the kitchen door holding a pitcher of water. She looked at the two and briskly announced,

"Dinner is served!" She set down the pitcher, and Renee started to fill the glasses at the table. Then the two disappeared into the kitchen, and brought out the chicken, beans, and bread basket. Renee found a gravy bowl in the cabinet and brought that out last with a bowl of mashed potatoes, and Tabitha lit the two candles on the table. The sun was just starting to set, and she shut the front window wooden shutters to block out the sun to let the candlelight cast a golden glow over the table.

Luke had seated Renee, and now came over to seat his daughter across from her. He took the head-of-the-table chair, in between the two.

Smiling, Tabitha held up her glass for a pour. She'd had champagne before, and felt very grown up tonight.

Renee asked, "Shall we say grace?"

Luke and Tabitha looked at each other.

They both said yes together, and Renee led with a simple prayer.

"Thank you, Lord, for this wonderful food, good company and being able to gather together for this meal. Amen."

The two repeated,

"Amen."

What followed was a delicious and highly-conversational meal. It was as if they each felt already so comfortable together, even though this was their first meal together. Renee lauded Tabitha on her efficient help at the school. Luke commented on the house improvements with her touch as being just what the house needed. He added he was trying to put his office into better order himself. He sat back with a sigh.

"This dinner is the best I have ever had, I believe!" Tabitha beamed.

"Well, I could not have done any of it without Renee's help. She knows so much about cooking!" Renee laughed.

"It came by necessity, but you're an able student!"

Renee offered to clear when everyone was full, and as she started, Tabitha noticed her father could not take his eyes off of her as she walked around the table, collecting plates. She smiled knowingly, and stood to help out. Then the three moved the conversation to the outside porch, with Tabitha taking the top step as usual, and Luke and Renee sitting side-by-side on the bench.

It was a beautiful night, and they all gazed at the dark sky filled with stars, breathing in the cooling air.

"We still have dessert!" Tabitha chimed.

"I'll try it, but I won't be able to eat much, I'm pretty full!" Luke rubbed his stomach.

"Well, you better try!" said Tabitha.

She stood and stretched. "I'll go get it ready to serve."

She left the two alone, and went into the kitchen, sure to take her time in cutting three slices and plating each. Meanwhile, the two sitting close to each other were silent, looking out again into the night.

"How long is the drive to your place?" Luke asked her, thinking about her riding the wagon back alone in the dark.

"About thirty minutes. I have a lantern with me, so I'll be fine."

"I'm not wanting you to ride alone, or leave at all, I must admit." They turned toward each other.

"I don't want to either..." Luke took her hand, and their mouths touched gently in a kiss, and they breathed sighs of pleasure. Luke pulled away and spoke into her neck.

"I like you very much, Renee."

"I feel the same way."

"I... haven't been with anyone in... years."

"Same..."

"So, we're two amateurs, huh?" They both laughed.

"I guess so!"

He took her cheeks gently with both hands.

"I think you're wonderful. I want to know you."

"I think it's mutual, my dear."

Tabitha called through the open door,

"Dessert's ready!"

Luke held her hand as they rose and entered the dining room once again. Tabitha was sitting, and was chewing on a bite of pie. She closed her eyes and said,

"Mmmmm-mmmmm!" She opened her eyes and looked at Renee, nodding.

Renee floated to her seat, totally wrapped up in the moment and the feelings of budding love, for both of these newfound friends in her rather lone and simple life. It now felt as though she'd come upon immense happiness all at once. She savored the moment the rest of the evening.

An hour later, even though Luke asked her again if he shouldn't accompany her home, she insisted on a solo trip, changed into her riding duds, and got hugs from Tabitha before carrying her dress to the wagon, while Luke was hooking up her horse.

"I had the best time of my life tonight, thank you so much for making it so special!"

"I think you are the one who made it special!" Both ladies grinned widely, knowing her unspoken meaning.

"Are you . . . comfortable...with your father...and I...?"

"Yes, Renee."

"You are an amazing young lady; more mature than most people I know. I can tell your father loves you very much and cares about what your feelings are.

"I want him to be happy. I want you to be happy!"

"See you soon, then?" Renee picked up her wrapped dress and bag.

"See you soon, then."

Outside, Luke was awaiting Renee with her wagon all ready to go. He took her bag for her and stored it in the back. She lay her dress carefully down. Luke held her in the partial moonlight, and she leaned against him for a time. They kissed, long and passionately. He whispered he'd come by the next day to see her. She kissed his nose and let him easily lift her up onto the bench. He waved at her just before she was out of sight and sighed loudly.

He was a man in love.

Later as Renee walked into her house, she felt like a different woman. Paul was already asleep in his room, as the door was closed, and she took off her clothes and lay naked under her blankets. She held herself, closing her eyes, thinking about Luke. She felt his mouth, his hands, and wanted him. She fell asleep easily, smiling as she slipped into a beautiful dream.

Waiting...

The next morning, Luke walked out to the barn as usual, and was surprised by a visitor. Aditsan was sitting on a hay bale with crossed arms, with one of his men standing behind him.

"My friend!" Luke came forward and the two hugged briefly. Their horses were standing behind them, tied up to a post. "Come into the house for some food. I won't take no for an answer." The three went inside, and sat at the table, while Luke quickly made a pot of coffee. Tabitha still had not come down yet.

The three sat around the table, and no one spoke. Luke was used to this silence with his friend. He brought out the rest of the bread and butter from last night's meal. He motioned for them to eat and drink and awaited Aditsan's verbal reason for the visit.

"There is trouble. We are in trouble. I need your help." Luke studied his face, and it held fear and anger.

"Anything you need, of course. Yes."

The conversation lasted for longer than Luke had ever spoken with his friend before. Aditsan spoke, at first with anger, then with fear at length about his problem. Luke listened patiently, then asked questions to further understand and clarify if what he meant was what he himself was in fear of. It would require him leaving home for a period of time, duration not known, which he preferred not to do at this time. It would mean personal danger for him, and his friend, and he had just found his family and his love and had no desire to leave. But this was his blood brother of a kind, of fate's creation, and he was compelled to answer the call.

Apparently, according to Aditsan, the Apache chief had assembled warriors and were planning on an attack in the north to capture land that the Navajo held but which overlapped into New Mexico territory that was occupied already by the Apaches. They had sent scouts who were painted with their war colors of red and black. They'd assumed the land would not be ceded and were already prepared for battle. But there was a twist in just another skirmish between tribes.

Apparently, there was a political figurehead, a White Man making promises to the Apache tribe leaders to allow them to expand their borders by ridding much of Arizona of all other tribes who held land that they were not willing to cede to the White Man. Luke would do research and investigate exactly who this man or men were, and could then seek help from the Governor's office in Phoenix, unless...and this would be devastating...they were part of the coup. That would mean US military troops becoming involved, and that would mean certain death for many tribes, including the Apache and obviously the Navajo.

His head was spinning from it all, as it was a tragedy from out of left field he never saw coming. It would take swift and sure action to handle, but with little information, Luke was afraid of the outcome. All he knew for sure was that he must help out his friend.

After eating, and making preliminary plans, they clapped hands and would meet at the designated day and time. As he watched them leave on their mustangs, riding behind his house and into the trees, his heart was heavy.

He heard his daughter in the kitchen, and sighed deeply, not knowing what he was going to say to her. He also needed to talk with Renee. He had much to do that day. Trying to make sense of it all would have to wait.

The two had a small breakfast, and saddled up both horses. They went for a short ride so Luke could show her how the well worked to provide them with water at the far end of their property. As they rode out, he explained things to her about where to get what in town, and who to talk to for supplies or services. He explained to her that he had to leave for a time, but would be back as soon as he could work it out. He told her if there were any problems, she could stay with Renee, who would board Bandit in her barn. The two of them were to come back to the property every three days to check on things and get what she might need.

Tabitha was such a mature young lady for a sixteen-year-old, and did not appear distressed. She asked a lot of questions he provided answers to as simply as he could, without saying anything that may confuse her.

"I'm happy to stay with Renee, but I also want to keep things up here. Now, show me how the kitchen pump draws water from the well." Luke smiled as she dismounted Bandit to begin the lesson about cast iron pressure pumps.

She needn't have any chaperone at all, but he'd feel better if Renee knew she was safe.

He packed up for camping out, brought two rifles and two pistols with ammo. He hugged his daughter fully and kissed her cheek.

"You should be careful in all that you do, and know that I will be back."

"I will be here."

"Tab, I love you."

No one had ever called her that, and she held him again.

"Father, I love you too." She felt tears coming to her.

"Daughter, you are the most important person in my life. Never forget that, even though we didn't spend so many years together...I'm so sorry that...our life apart... happened..."

"It was her decision; you didn't even know I existed..."

It was the first they spoke of their years of being apart which had been out of their control. It killed Luke to have to undergo a second one, now that he had her in his life. He pulled away, and mounted up, forcing himself to go and make the meeting with Aditsan. He headed towards

Renee's on the Angus Cattle Company ranch, and he blinked back tears of his own...

It was late morning when he arrived at the house Renee had given him directions to. She was tending to something at the side of the house. He felt his heart flip and she looked up, hearing Charlotte ride up and whinny. She waved at him and started to walk up to the dirt path. She held some wildflowers she had been cutting and held them at her side. She wore an oversized white tee shirt she had tied around her waist. She wore blue jeans with the cuffs rolled up and looked like a young girl. Her hair was caught up at the back with a clip with curly tendrils escaping around her smiling face. He tied up and the two held each other and kissed as if they had been together forever.

She greeted Charlotte by rubbing her short nose, then watered at the wooden trough at the post. Then she led her love to the porch, and inside the door.

He waited while she put the flowers in a glass vase on the kitchen table. She came over to him, and looked up shyly.

"Paul won't be home until dark. Can you stay awhile?" Luke burned for her.

He whispered into her ear, "Try and stop me."

They gently, at first gingerly, then passionately made love on Renee's fluffy down bed. They took their time, touching each other everywhere, appreciating each other's bodies, and how well they fit together. She was not shy and she opened up to him immediately, as it wasn't difficult for her since coming to know him to trust this man with all of her heart.

Tears came to her eyes as she felt the connection to him in a way, she'd never experienced this level of intimacy before. He looked at her in awe, and told her,

"Renee, I love you." She gasped to get a deep enough breath to respond.

"You must know I do too."

The heat was on that day and even though the sun was starting to set, they lay on top of the covers, waiting for a breeze from the window at the headboard of the four-poster bed. They faced each other, touching, talking, basking in their new love. There were no sounds besides the ones they themselves made. Renee lit two candles on either side of her bed. They lay as long as they dare, and then rose and dressed, anticipating Paul's arrival home.

Sitting in her kitchen sipping water, Luke looked at her seriously. They held hands across the table.

"I need to leave Prescott for a time, I'm not sure for how long. I don't want to alarm you...it could be that there will be some trouble for my friend I need to help out." She squeezed his hand.

"Tell me..."

"You remember my friend Aditsan...he's having a problem with Apache rivals and needs help...White help...my help. He's...like my brother, and I want to help him and his people if I can.

"I won't tell you everything is going to be fine but I will tell you I am always careful. And now...I have two big reasons to stay safe...you, and my daughter."

"I... I understand...I will worry, but I need to know the truth. What can I do to help?"

"You can check on Tab, or she can stay here, or...you could stay there if you like. I just want to know that she is safe."

"Yes, of course. She...will help keep my mind occupied!" She nodded. "Where...will you be?"

"Up north. I... have to leave tonight. I hate leaving you both right now...but I will return...I promised her and I promise you. Nothing can keep me away for long...and I trust Aditsan with my life."

"Well, then I have to trust him with your life too."

"I don't want to leave you…" Luke stood and so did she, and they embraced. She touched his face.

"Please, be careful…I have so much to tell you…to show you…to do with you…" Her voice trailed off, and he kissed her again, with a fervor neither of them had experienced before…and he had to rip himself away and take off into the night. She couldn't see him within seconds, and she said a silent prayer up to the sky. She went inside to start some kind of dinner, not at all sure of what she would be making. There was no chance she would be falling to sleep easily that night anytime soon.

Dreams Come True . . .

Luke had acute vision at night, maybe because of how many times he'd traveled without sunlight. His horse was also the most sure-footed animal he'd ever experienced riding on. He made his way north, not needing any sleep. At first daylight, he met at the rendezvous point, early, but of course, three Navajo braves were already awaiting his arrival. Aditsan was not with them.

They all three nodded at Luke, then quickly turned and led him down the White Mesa rising down into Kaibito Canyon. They carried no firearms. As he rode with them with peak awareness of who he rode with...and the danger that it presented, his daughter's face and Renee's eyes floated through his mind, and he started sweating. What the hell was he doing?

High Noon

It was high noon by the time they came up to the camp deep in the North Kaibito Canyon, a good place to keep under cover. There was the smell of a smoke in the air and the braves were eating, not making a campfire in the night that could be easily seen from far away.

As they rode up, the braves made a whooping call that was answered with another, as if exchanging a secret code to allow entry without alarm. Luke spied his brother and felt grateful that he was alive and well.

After food and water, a tepee had been erected for Luke, who needed rest after being up for 36 hours. He slept quickly and easily for four hours. When night fell, he stretched out and joined the small band around the two torches for light.

There was low talking in the Navajo language between the men. Luke understood very little.

"We have Apache trouble as usual. But this time it is led by a White Man l ast attack loft fifteen dead. They are trying to gain lost land White Man steals. I ask you to help fight White Man as White Man. An Army man from the war between the states has agreed to meet with you to talk about working out a treaty to stop the killing. He knew your father."

Silence passed. Luke thought over his proposal.

Luke was aware of the aggression Whites had imposed upon local tribes in the many territories they had come across, as a "call to expansion" that the eastern politicians had enacted.

The explosion of the Great Western Expansion had begun post-Civil War in 1865, with, "40 Acres and a Mule" Order, for free slaves in the deep south. General Sherman proposed this plan and Lincoln approved it. This unprecedented Order seemingly allowed the negro people (non-Caucasian) to be able to settle on their own land that was deemed their property. Tragically, the land was later sharecropped, given back to the former landowners who had fought for the Confederacy against the Union side of the war. Most freed men and women were left to survive on their own; many starved to death or were otherwise killed. The promise of free land influenced thousands to claim the acreage and a lent mule, and work the land. But the land turned out to not be really theirs.

The Native Americans proposed no ownership of their land. They lived, for the most part, in peace; they didn't build fences around their communities to keep their women and children safe. They didn't build permanent abodes. But with the influx of firearms as well as military support, armed forts settled along the way with high wooden walls surrounding their bases to prevent and protect them from attack and maintain possession and presence on their "captured" property.

The Civil War was a war of profit. Slavery allowed the White Man to pay nothing if little by forcing field labor for natural resources to be grown and manufactured during a budding agricultural and pre-industrial era.

The Nations of the country never made such a stand, they only continued to make their own way on the vast acreage that was America. The land afforded fresh water, forests, beasts of various kinds, ore to be mined, rich soil to grow vegetables and fruit and wheat for ample food. White families settling in this new territorial area would make a natural army of populations to grow and control these riches for generations to come, but their greed made the difference in their procurement.

The Western European peoples that settled in the very first thirteen colonies were much more knowledgeable and sophisticated than the primitive Native. However, from the first White Men's steps onto the shore of Massachusetts, they recognized the rich resources that spread further than the eye could see that they had never even dreamed existed, given their smaller individual homelands.

On the way west, Native responses among different tribes to the thousands of western-bound pioneers, including trappers, cattlemen, farmers, lumbermen, and speculators who'd heard of the gold being panned in certain areas was bound to cause extreme and sudden tensions. The Sutter Mill gold strike in California started a "gold fever" and mines were found of gold, silver and copper in southern Arizona.

Thus, what followed were the American-Indian Wars, starting around 1850, and ending in 1886...over thirty years of raids, brutal killings and massacres, including women and children of both Whites and Natives.

History books tell us the Apache were vicious warriors that thought nothing of slaughtering children and women, as well as many young warriors of surrounding tribes. They were called "The Great Marauders" of the Wild West, foe to civilian and military White Men.

This was a true tragedy, and this was also true of other tribes, and the White Man himself. If threatened, in any community where law is not present, where greed and abundance coexist, there follows power conflicts, and thus death...death that seems unreasonable and unnecessary by each side of the conflict.

There are remnants of a Sinagua village built between 1125 and 1400 A.D. The adobe buildings have two stories. Archeologists have surmised by the discovery that there was no preparatory plan for the buildings; rooms were added as necessary, probably due to their population increase. Few doors were found to have been installed and used, but ladders were to access the roof's many trapdoor openings in the local tree-branch coverings of the adobe for entrance into each room. Walls were made of limestone and sandstone; roof supports and coverage was made of juniper, pine, and cottonwood trees, indigenous to the high desert. There were an estimated eighty-six rooms in all, fifteen of which were upstairs, accommodating approximately 225 men, women and children. This treasure of history would become a National Monument in 1940, and is near the town of Clarkdale. The people were of the Navajo Nation.

This village was standing perhaps 600 years before the travels of Christopher Columbus; 400 years before the first colony from England was ever settled. This land was most assuredly their land.

The Navajo had always been peaceful, except when pressed to rebound from external attacks. The Apache may have been slower to consider peace when threatened...especially when as a people they were confronted and killed over and over again as the White Man treaties were broken—repeatedly. They started calling the natives the Red Man. His skin under the sun without the clothing trappings easterners wore daily gave him a terra cotta color, like the earth in Arizona, New Mexico and Utah. The Red Rock Canyons in the Sedona area and the mesas and pyres standing huge in the deserts reflected the Native American exactly...they'd been the first inhabitants. They were there to stay, and the color was as if of a mixture of Earth and blood...many deaths due to the White Man expansion occurred, without being documented, but those who were still present to survive their influx were witnesses who remembered.

Apache and Comanche natives perhaps became the more aggressive tribes as a survival method, especially when they held up carved stone arrowheads against rifles and pistols. There were also reports of virus epidemics due to European diseases never present before like mumps, measles, chicken pox and scarlet fever. Typhus, cholera and influenza were also a reason for many deaths.

The American-Indian wars began by the White Man herding hundreds of Apache people to gather and live on what the American Government called an Apache Reservation, located in eastern Arizona. The land provided shelter, protection and food at no cost to the natives. It seemed like a perfect alternative to territorial wars breaking out for mere survival between the two sides.

Unfortunately, settlers in southern Arizona banded together and murdered most of the natives while they were living all together in one area. The Apache simply retaliated.

This was known as the Camp Grant Massacre.

Geronimo's rise and defeat, ending in his surrender in 1886 halted the exacerbating Apache raids. As the story goes, upon coming home to his encampment somewhere in an eastern Arizona canyon, he came upon the ashes of his entire family. There was evidence of the White Man's presence, and he gathered a small army to revolt for many years. He was captured but escaped many times. With the appointment of Sheriff Andrew Slaughter whose sole purpose became bringing about order to this wild territory, he actually aided in stabilizing the law in the area after the situation settled down.

But Geronimo had an ally in a White Man who happened to be jealous of Slaughter's fame and progress...his younger brother, Albert. This man made a conscious decision to become a "spy" of a sort...supposedly helping in the capture of the famous Chief, but actually aiding the Apache in their continued skirmishes against not the Whites, but the Navajo, Pima and Hopi. Just as there were Native trackers working for them, this seemed to be the opposite of this system, and to be either was considered the most traitorist work for any man, and grounds for hanging; probably torture if a Native was caught tracking against their own kind and certainly execution for a White traitor.

Removal of 60,000 natives from their homes occurred decades earlier of mostly members of the Cherokee Nation when the US Government allocated land west of the Mississippi River to be designated as Indian Territory, but it was just a way to force them from the development in the southeast area of the US as early as 1830. They were forced to march, and almost 20,000 died along the treacherous trek, due to starvation, thirst and exposure to the elements.

Geronimo was held by the US Military as a prisoner of war as a result of his conditional surrender in 1886. He had been persistent in fighting any people who tried to take away land belonging to the Apache tribe, which stretched from New Mexico to Arizona.

There were also Mexicans involved in the disputes. Mormons were responsible for a religious movement against persecution based on beliefs. Many combined forces to survive and thrive, including some of the White population with non-white; of that group, Luke Richmond was certainly a part.

He had heard enough. His brother Aditsan had shared late into the night, and when all others, except his always-present "flank warriors" who protected him with their lives, had gone to their shelters.

He took his brother's hand in unity.

"What do you want me to do?"

"Have a meeting with this Albert. White Man to White Man." They shook hands.

Aditsan and Luke

Renee and Tabitha were having tea at lunch at the first downtown Prescott restaurant, The Palace Saloon, which was solely a bar featuring card tables beside the long, polished pinewood bar with matching wooden stools. Then the owners bought out the building next to theirs in order to expand the saloon into an actual restaurant. On the second floor, there had been rooms to rent.

The two ladies sat by the window and enjoyed the sunny day. It had been four days since Luke had left town. Without saying the exact words, Renee felt it was important to share with his daughter sitting across from her the reality of her relationship with Luke.

"I... enjoy your father's company very much, as I enjoy yours. I think...I may have very strong feelings for him."

"I absolutely know he has the same feelings for you, I can tell, and I think it's a good thing." Renee smiled. "For both of you!"

"I'm so glad to hear you say that. I'm also glad we have each other while he is away." She took the young lady's hand across the table, and they both squeezed the others.

Tabitha decided after lunch to walk down to the Sheriff Office to check on things, though never prompted to do so by her father. His deputies were both nice gentlemen, in their twenties, and not very talkative. They mostly asked her questions about eastern life, and how she found their western ways. She could only share a limited amount of information due to the fact that she was not quite aware of how ordinary life was in Philadelphia and New York City. She only knew prestigious restaurants, events, haute couture, and an ivy league education. But they were charming, not to be looked down upon as her mother may have done years before.

Renee was keeping busy with school work and at home, but she also wished she could talk with Luke. There would be no ability to reach him as he would be camping out, location unknown. She knew for her to stay busy would be important so as not to dwell and worry about what Luke was engaged in.

During the day that worked. During the night, however, in the great, dark long silence that surrounded her the moment she tucked herself in bed, she breathed deeply, closed her eyes, and her thoughts were impossible to halt.

She touched the pillow next to her where he'd laid his head, underneath the covers where he'd slept on her white cotton sheets. She turned on her side and stroked where his back and side had touched. She closed her eyes again and saw his face, his eyes, felt his breath on her skin, and moaned in his absence. Then she saw him riding away quickly from her as if he found their separation painful. She didn't want to, but a tear escaped from her eye and dropped onto her pillow. She missed him...her love...her Luke.

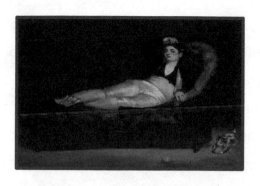

Goya's "Lady on Settee"

Sophia looked at the clock as she drank her second glass of Claret. She sat on her red velvet settee in the parlor, gazing out the picture windows at her beautiful garden. Her husband and she had barely spoken to one another since Tabitha's absence, and when they did it was at morning coffee and at dinner, when he made it home. She'd been suspicious of his accruing time spent away from home, and her feeling was it could be because of another woman he had preferred to spend time with. She'd been privy to some rumors, gossip, and concern from her mother, who hired a private investigator to track Randolph. She was awaiting her mother who was joining her for a 5:00 pm cocktail, though she had already started without her.

Finally, the doorbell chimed, and her mother entered the salon, led in by Pierre, her forever French butler, concierge, and lately confidante.

Mother was dressed in her usual finery, still very attractive in her late fifties. She eyed the wine on the table in the decanter. She gracefully removed her Reboux hat, her Walton lace gloves, and crossed over in her Louis IV heeled shoes to the opposite beige velvet settee. Her French Couture blue-lace gown rustled from the myriad of petticoats underneath.

She almost looked like a stranger to Sophia, as it had been many weeks since her mother had come over for a visit. Margaret York, pale and petite, sat herself delicately on the seat, carefully crossing her ankles in front of her. Her eyes were cast down.

"I see you've started without me, dear." She looked to Pierre, who'd followed her inside the room and stood at the ready at the credenza on the opposite wall.

"Pierre, I'll have a Dubonnet with a twist of lemon."

Sophia sat awaiting her mother's first sip from the crystal glass, and Pierre exited the salon quietly. Margaret placed the glass on the lace doily and folded her tiny hands in her lap, breathing in and out slowly. She finally looked at her daughter directly, until Sophia was forced to meet the blue-eyed glare.

"Darling, how are you feeling?"

"Mother, just tell me." Sophia drained her glass. She just wanted the truth.

"Well..." Her mother frowned, "Really! No pleasantries?"

Sophia sighed loudly.

"No. Just tell me. Is he cheating on me?"

Silence filled the room as she watched her mother drink another sip of Dubonet. She grimaced at seemingly the drink, and set it down, pushing it away as if beneath her.

She reached into her Hermes beaded bag beside her, and opened up the gold-plated clasp. She retrieved a letter, and placed it on the table between them. Her eyes downcast, she awaited her daughter's reaction.

Sophia took it and opened the tri-folded letter. She read silently the report her mother had acquired for her. It was typed and signed by the head of the detective agency, Mr. Robert Burke.

June 29, 1890

Dear Mrs. Randolph Martin,

After three weeks of investigation of both documents and physical search, I have come to the following conclusion:

Mr. Randolph Martin has been at the following locations with the following individuals at the dates and time noted below:

6.6.90:	2889 5th Ave.	6:00pm - 9:00pm
6.7.90	2889 5th Ave.	6:00pm - 9:00 pm
6.8.90:	2889 5th Ave.	6:00pm - 9:00pm
6.11.90	2889 5th Ave.	6:00pm - 9:00 pm
6..1290:	2889 5th Ave.	6:00pm - 9:00pm
6.13.90	2889 5th Ave.	6:00pm - 9:00 pm
6.16.90:	2889 5th Ave.	6:00pm - 9:00pm
6.17.90	2889 5th Ave.	6:00pm - 9:00 pm
6.18.90:	2889 5th Ave.	6:00pm - 9:00pm
6.19.90	2889 5th Ave.	6:00pm - 9:00 pm
6.20.90:	2889 5th Ave.	6:00pm - 9:00pm
6.21.90	2889 5th Ave.	6:00pm - 9:00 pm

Each incident occurred with one Mrs. Lillian Annabelle Leary-MacMurphy, wife of Mr. Patrick Lee MacMurphy., residing at 1616 New Haven Drive, Long Island, NY. The address is of the 5th Avenue Hotel of New York City. The Room Number was 1210.

Remittance statement attached.

Mr. Robert Burke, LLC.
New York, New York

Sophia stared at the letter on thick stationery using brown ink in small font lettering for what seemed like several minutes. She reread the dates and times. She reread her husband's name. She reread the name of the individual he'd met with for three hours, every three evenings in a row, with two days in between.

She did not recognize the name. She did not recognize the address. She did recognize the Avenue, though she knew the best hotels in the city were in that area.

She looked up at her mother, who was studying her face for the first time since she'd arrived. Sophia was speechless. Her mother, however, had a lot to say.

"Darling, Mr. Burke is a reputable man, he used to be a police officer and was recommended to me by several of your father's friends. He's also discreet so rest assured no one will ever hear about this outside of our family. Papa wants to meet with you to discuss what and how to handle this situation. Then he wants to meet with Randolph.

She nodded her head in a numb daze. Even though she was suspicious, it was only real now that it had been written down.

In an instant, all thought of her breaking out on her own, joining her daughter out west, and getting back at her cheating husband disappeared from thought.

"I only know he has to do the right thing."

"Yes, dear, it's true. Now we know he has to do the right thing. Agreed?"

Margaret sipped again at her drink, draining the glass. Sophia poured herself another glass of wine. Both women had every intention of making this situation come out to their advantage.

Claret Wine Goblet, Dorflinger, 1860

Besides the dark magenta, terra cotta and gold in desert sunsets, the sunrise as the yellow ball rose from the east was also breathtaking, in lighter hues of apricot, dark blue, and brilliant flaxen. Luke almost always viewed it from his ranch porch. At the encampment he was staying at, there were no tall trees, so much more of the sky was exposed. Kaibito Plateau lay in the northeast area of the state, just west of Apache country. They were camping in a small canyon, with a creek that ran through it, feeding off the Colorado River north of them. There was local game for food, and the Navajos knew the area well. It had been about a week since he had left his home and he thought of his daughter and Renee often, especially early mornings and before sleeping for the night.

They were a small band of about twenty. Scouts were sent out and came back with any news of Apache sightings in the area or encampments. So far, the enemy was laying low, nowhere in sight. Adistan had been awaiting word from the Apache chief about the meeting with Albert, the famous Sheriff's younger brother, and Luke.

It had been just a few months ago, on March 7th, when an Apache raid north of Globe broke out against the US Military troops who were aggressively trying to oust the tribe within the Arizona Territory northeast.

The Apache Kid and Masai were some of the men who held out after Geronimo had been sent east by Lieutenant Powhatan Clarke of the 10th Cavalry. He had hired military and scouts of other tribes to return the raiding led by these two Apache warriors. The "Gray Fox" Crook was the "Hero of the Settlers" because of his forceful barrage of the Apache and other marauders into settler's communities.

President Grant called all of this, "the American Indian Problem." He sent out aides to help pressure the tribes to move onto reservations, allocated land set aside land for them and their families to live...a boundary life on government terms. They provided food, shelter and safety for their own allocation of most of the land.

Lt. Col. Crook, c. 1881

Apparently, about nine years before Luke had his
misgivings about what was about to transpire, Lt. Colonel
Crook had been moved back east. An underling of his was
Lieutenant Henry Slaughter. He'd helped in moving
Apaches onto reservations working out of Fort Apache,
about 500 miles east of Prescott, but he'd also kept in touch
with several Apache former tribe leaders who escaped
incarceration, and had hid out in New Mexico. These braves
coaxed any and all leftover Apache to join their squad of

sorts, and to attach themselves to Slaughter meant easier access to guns, which meant power. Of course, their plan could not be to attack the military or government which had obviously made their presence and power known. There was no fighting and winning against that machine. But there was land to be found far north in Arizona, held presently by the Navajo.

Slaughter outlined a plan to attack the tribes there, which had weakened over the years due to the Whitemen, and then form their own tribal hybrid to stand apart from reservation control.

Sadly, Slaughter could care less about these outliers, and only wanted to provide his paycheck signers, the US Army, more and more and as much as possible in the way of land, and tragically Army Scouts, which were in most cases unpaid soldiers.

Slaughter was a transplant from the east. Like Luke, his family raised horses in New York. He had met and done business with another equine businessman, Luke's father. He was about ten years older than Luke, and a likable person, and the two got on well. When he found out Luke, John's son was a lawman in Prescott, researched by his contacts. Tribes of different types communicated with each other constantly, and somehow a certain Sheriff had done some business with a Chief of importance of a large tribe of Navajo.

This was quite a revelation for the Lieutenant, only six months before, as he sat on his porch, smoking his cigar, listening to his wife chirping away with their daughter inside their Tucson home. He thought long and hard about this for most of the evening, and as he answered his wife's call to supper being ready, he stood up knowing what his little brother Albert would do. But for now, he put out his cigar, and entered his house, putting on his biggest grin as he made his way to the table.

Believing the meeting was imperative to survival, Aditsan wanted this to take place in his territory, with his men armed and ready. That would mean using scouts who would have to send word by horseback which would take days.

Aditsan insisted they hold their ground, and sent his two best scouts on the best steeds. He did not trust the American government, nor the military to be fair and allow the Navajo entitlement to their present land acreage. He felt if his feet were on its ground, it was safer to call this land his people's rightful home.

Nights were spent by torches and a circle of men talking low and seriously about the acquisition of ammo, more men, more horses, and strategies of war in case a fight ensued. Aditsan wanted peace above all, but was willing to answer to the potential aggression. Apaches usually fought first and retreated to plan later. But what about the "afterwards" of this is what was on the Navajo's mind, and what land would be truly theirs in the end?

Luke's mind as he lay down to sleep on his roll was far from any of this...it was back with his daughter and his love...

Lake Wilson, Prescott

Tabitha kept herself very busy during her father's absence. She counted the days on the kitchen wall calendar, marking out each day as it passed. He'd left June 20th, and it was now July 1st. She felt his absence and would have been very lonely were it not for Renee, Bandit and Margaret, her neighbor. She cleaned every room, scrubbing the wooden floors and rugs, polishing the furniture with oil, washing and hanging sheets, towels, and clothing in the back, where the washer stood on four legs with a crank-operated wringer. She cleaned the kitchen cabinets and washed unused dishes and pans. She practiced cooking and baking different things. She arranged a small library of the books remaining from Renee's library in the parlor. She polished mirrors with newspaper and vinegar. She weeded the small flower bed in front and bought seeds to grow more. Raking the entire front flower bed, she brought rocks from the surrounding land to border the beds and organized the planting.

She'd gone shopping, alone and with Renee and purchased catalog garments and accessories. She rode Bandit daily, and kept scouting the border of their property to explore the perimeters. She would see wildlife of coyotes, bobcats, deer and various rodents, mostly running and head-bobbing Quail with up to eight babies fluttering behind the mother. She'd never seen these before, nor Roadrunners. She made a note to do more research about indigenous animals in Renee's encyclopedia collection.

She'd gotten two letters from her mother since she'd been gone. The first told her to contact her straight away to let her know she was safe (by telegram). The second was the surprise...her mother Sophia sounded better in spirit, a little lighter, and was taking part in more activities with other women in her city. She didn't mention Randolf at all. She assured Tabitha she was fine with her staying out west for as long as she wanted to, and always to contact her if she needed anything. Tab knew her mother loved her, was devoted to her life and safety, and she felt that same way about Sophia.

Renee went back and forth between her house on the Angus Ranch and Luke's ranch. She called on Tab almost every day, as she had the entire month of June free of students. They had long talks, and rode their horses together, shopped and shared meals. They even hiked and went swimming at Watson Lake.

They spent some of their time making the school rooms look pleasant and more academically themed; they cleaned, painted, procured donated furniture, a new heating stove, and another blackboard for another wall. After the district stipend was used, Tab, who had an ample trust fund from her parents, donated to get quality and brand-new materials for the students. They ordered handwriting books and reference books, alphabet templates, and hanging maps of Arizona, the United States, and the world, along with classroom globe. Some basic Science kits appealed to Tab. Both women enjoyed choosing from the catalogs at the Mercantile together. Renee was so grateful for Tab's contributions that she later honored her with a school fund for other donors to contribute under her name.

Paul, Renee's brother was immensely helpful with his handyman skills, muscle-strength and his sense of humor. The three made a lively trio when they worked together, and it was a good way for both to use their time and not worry so much about Luke.

Renee and Tab were eating dinner in Tab's dining room, discussing the town celebration for the fourth of July weekend, starting with the rodeo. The fairgrounds on the west side of the town had an arena, with wood benches and an oval dirt field for the games. It was a lively show for all. Barbeque tables were set up with food for horse and bull riders, as well as spectators. In fact, well-known riders came from New Mexico, Texas and Colorado came to enter the Cowboy Contests for riding and roping. It would be the Third Annual Rodeo this year, with each July celebration getting bigger and brighter. They earned cash prizes, silver belt buckles, and there was a 1st place silver trophy for overall horse riding. The military cavalry from nearby Fort Whipple took part in the Gurley Avenue parade which was on July 3rd, that Friday morning.

There were dances, exhibits, a carnival and games for children and adults to play in for prizes. It was all about great fun, but also lured outsiders to their little town for an influx of business. Renee would make sure Tab participated, with her brother who handled some of the bulls and horse auctions at the end. Angus Ranch was a major sponsor of "The Oldest Rodeo in America" and aimed to provide any livestock needed.

There were booths with local gemstones, silver that Native Americans fashioned into jewelry that were truly unique and beautiful pieces for both men and women. There was also competition from miners and gold panners who sold gems and ore products to the natives, but at an exorbitant amount.

So, the natives took part in the White Man celebration by being servants, suppliers, and gave their time to make and sell products and only receiving a fraction of profit back. They were part of the "entertainment" to show up in feathered headdresses, dancing to their drums and singing music, but, it fed their families.

Navajo Chief c. 1890

Luke was more than a small-town sheriff; he kept in the loop about more than his Northern Arizona Yavapai County Seat of Prescott and the Enchanted Valley. He kept his ears open and eager to learn about the widespread native dilemma over most of the west at this time in history. White Men thought of their indigenous residents as if relics; to be hurried into some other placement so that they could live somewhere else without being a threat.

There were also many career outlaws and it was his job to keep out of his area or locked up in jail and then transferred to Phoenix. Now more than ever, he had an actual family to protect. Many of these miscreants hid out in outlying areas of the desert and could easily take advantage of homesteaders.

Then, there were the Native rebels; Geronimo, the aggressive Apache chief leading several tribal attacks; Alchesay, one of the first leaders of the Nation to be won over by the White man's side; he'd fallen under General George Crook's persuasive spell, a man who swore the Apache were merely "tenacious tigers" to be brought to submission by certain means, including employing the natives as "Indian Scouts," a softer name for traitor. This entailed offers of promised land and payment by Whites for changing sides.

Alchesay engaged in the patrol and management of the territory wanting full leader control, if only in his own mind, with the unspoken goal of taking over completely and reigning over all Chiefdom of any tribe habituating in the area. Building up this realm in manpower and maintaining a sure stronghold meant that Natives would be working under him. There was rarely payment from government, state and military coffers in American dollars, but usually the work was in trade for lodging, food and alcohol; perversely, Native American slavery was rampant, up into the mid-18th century. There were actual reports back east of Natives who

were persuaded to enslave Africans after the Civil War by southern rebel "Never Give
Up-ers."

The morning of July first, Luke knew there might be an "earthquake rumble" of tension about to shake the earth as more and more White Man oppression caused subjugation of proud Natives. He felt the resentment as if it were a heart pulse getting louder and faster. The Apache Kid had been making noise in the news and he was likely the leader of the land dispute against the Navajo. He had been in contact with Lieutenant Slaughter, or so it was rumored, and they were supposedly gaining traction, by acclamation of warriors and armaments as a result.

The scouts came back, finally. They spoke with Aditsan and Luke. A meeting was happening that evening, just before dusk.

No specific names of the opposition were spoken, only the place and time, shown by a simple sundial on a low hill nearby. The ten Navajo braves were armed with rifles, knives and bow outfits strapped across their backs. Twenty of them would arrive that evening at Sand Springs, not far from their camp.

Luke would try any reasoning methods with the Slaughter, while Aditsan would speak the language of the Apaches which he had learned from his father with Alchesay. They had always wanted peace, but the Apaches had broken many pacts in the past. These men held many resentments, and Luke could feel it.

The ride started with whoops and calls of confidence and excitement from the braves who carried their weapons and supplies behind them as they rode bareback with deft experience. They wore no paint on their faces or chests. They were young, fit and energetic men. They were virile, and after days of remaining hidden and undercover, they were now loud and boisterous, fearless against the night, ready for anything to happen.

Aditsan rode silently, filled with his thoughts and focused on the task at hand. He and Luke spoke, but very little. Luke knew that this meeting could turn into a melee of brutal bloody fighting, injuries, death...anything. There was no guarantee the Apaches would choose a peace treaty.

Sandy Springs was in the high desert with a trickling river. The core of the group met atop the highest crest of a nearby cliff, for visual advantage of surveying the area; two scouts went into the outlying grounds to find the Apache group.

Luke felt a change in the air, and he felt it in his gut which was rarely wrong. Beads of sweat fell down from underneath his hat onto his face. He kept saying to himself,

"You now have reason to live."

He'd tolerated several days of not knowing what would come to pass, and sleepless nights feeling his heart bump inside his chest with images of Renee and his daughter in his head. He was happy for all this to be over, and Charlotte alerted him with her neigh when he heard hooves of horses pounding toward them.

Aditsan met the opposing scouts with his men as Luke stepped up slowly behind the group. They were to mount up and follow.

They met in the "Manuai" tepee, a huge dome-shaped dwelling with an interior ceiling over ten feet high. Luke sat at the right of Aditsan with a fire centered in the circle of Natives. An opening at the tip of the animal skins and pine canes made the interior like a sweathut, and Luke took off his hat and gloves. It was an extraordinary event that had taken place.

Geronimo years before had taken his tribe warriors to the Whites. He'd become deputized as a Head Scout of the Apaches by General Cook and wanted to persuade all tribes in the Arizona-New Mexico area to work with the Army to instill peace and prosperity for all. The problem with that for the Navajo was that all of their land was up for grabs to keep the peace between the Natives and the White population; however, they, the Natives, were behind a red eight ball. The promise of land and food and arms and alcohol continued to be the reason for their supplication under the White Man, when in fact, this is the very reason they were cursed. There was no savior to tell them otherwise. They were giving in to the new population who brought rifles and construction and ideas that were far beyond their simple natural living existence. They had no cogent reason to resist. And so, Luke did not trust the scouting party words of courage.

Suddenly there was a commotion outside and into the huge tent strode three White Men and the Apache liaison Alchesay. He was rather short, and wore White Man's clothing. The tall man in military garb with the two flanking him must have been Slaughter, who scanned the dark interior until his eyes fell upon the only White Man inside, who'd already been standing; Luke Richmond, who met his 6'2" stance.

Slaughter widely greeted him with a nod and his widest smile.

"Mr. Luke Richmond."

"Mr. Slaughter. Mighty nice to meet you. Shall we talk?"

Apache Abode c. 1890

There was something ashen about the complexion of the Lieutenant to Luke, as if he hadn't ridden a horse or been out in the sun for a good year. Supposedly still on active duty, living under the burning southwest sun, his appearance betrayed him.

The two crunched over stones and shrubs to another canvas tent without a cover for an entryway. It may have been army-made. There were a couple low-seat chairs made of canvas, a few boxes, a cot for sleeping with blankets, and a table with metal cups and a couple of opened bottles of whiskey. Slaughter allowed Luke to step inside before him, and both sat on the chairs. He grabbed one of the bottles and two glasses from a cardboard box underneath the table. He filled both in silence, offering one of the shots to Luke. Luke shook his head.

"I'd rather not, no offense."

Slaughter still had the friendly smile still pasted across his face.

"I'd rather you did. I'm the law in any state, I'm military. I don't make deals like this."

"What deal?" Luke asked him bluntly.

"Drink first." He still held the whiskey out to him.

Luke chose to take it and both men drained their glasses.

Slaughter sat back, putting the bottle down.

Luke repeated, "What deal?"

"We're here to make a very unique agreement together, you and I. I wouldn't offer my time or this . . . opportunity unless . . . it was very profitable, to us both, of course.

He closed his eyes and breathed in deeply.

"I am a member of the Fort Apache 6th Cavalry. Our current goal is to arrest and take into custody the Apache you and your Chief were seated with."

Luke was confused but kept silent, letting Slaughter speak and take another whiskey.

"However, some feel Chief Alchesay and his men could help out the government more if he were free to take more scouts and take more land."

Luke stared at him, not understanding him fully.

"Yes, that is what we're here to do, to bring the Navajo into our "New Nation" and keep the peace living together. The land and the Indians will have more together than separately, if yer Navajos agree."

Quietly, Luke contemplated the full meaning of what Slaughter was saying.

"Why would this help the government?"

Back came the grin on the Lieutenant's face. Luke remained silent, then his gut told him that this was not for any Indian good at all. There was a lie here and he would be in on it if he agreed.

"Well, they'll live on the land designated by our military, eventually the government. All of their basic needs will be taken care of. The skirmishes will cease. Good for us, good for them.

"They, of course, will agree to sign a formal treaty agreement drafted by the 6th Cavalry. It will be retroceded to the government for land management purposes, and . . . the Navajo and Apache will . . . continue to work and develop the land.

"You mean, they will give up their current land holdings and be forced to live on government-owned reservation land."

"Like I said, good for us, good for them. So, can you see why I need you to make this case with your bosom buddy in there?"

Luke was sick to his stomach, and the weapons strapped to the thirty or so Apaches, and probably stored in boxes somewhere in one of the other tepees were probably going to make it difficult for the Navajo to leave without the agreement, which is basically a lie; that they will own their land, when in fact they'll be ceding it over to the government by force from the military; their intention was to turn Navajo communities and property into forced labor camps using their own land!

"Is there any compensation to the Navajo at this time for the agreement?" Luke asked this, trying to make time enough for him to figure out the dilemma before him. He was sweating profusely now, and the ashen Slaughter appeared as cool as a cucumber, as if none of this made any difference to him.

"Well, eventually. They'll have housing, food and be able to earn money working."

"Why do you think I can convince him with this one meeting with you? The Navajo are proud people. They have lived here for centuries. They were never meant to live on fenced acreage and being told what to do. That's like putting a stallion in a cage. It is inhumane."

He was searching this foe's face and Slaughter now looked as if Luke were speaking Russian.

"Indians ain't no stallions, Luke. They are nothing but trouble to us. They are standing in the way of our expansion, our culture, and yes, our profit. Yours and mine. They are wasting what they have because they don't know any better. It's going to come down to "us" or "them", one way or the other. It's too late to go backwards to how it was."

Luke could not speak. Slaughter started to light a cigar. The lanterns had been lit as the darkness settled over the camp. His two companions who had been standing outside of their tent brought in two lanterns and put them on the table so a bright glow filled the space. Luke felt cornered and anxious but he sat stoic and did not move.

"This is going to happen, whether they agree of not. You see that, don't you?"

"We will need to return to our camp so we can talk, so that I can talk to Aditsan in his camp."

Luke stood.

Slaughter stood.

"You can all stay here; we have plenty of room."

"We will need to talk about it at a Navajo camp. It is just their way."

Luke sweated out the next moments. He had hopefully bought some time.

Slaughter took another whiskey. For the first time, his look turned sour.

"Agreed. We meet tomorrow. Here. Before noon, and then—we will come to you."

Luke nodded, then slowly turned to exit the tent. The cigar smoke was overwhelming and he swallowed back a cough.

"Until tomorrow."

Slaughter's low raspy voice followed him as Luke made strides to the main tent and called from outside on Aditsan.

"A-dit-zahn!"

His friend appeared, and searched Luke's face in the dark. He'd heard the urgency in his voice.

"We go back to camp. Now."

Aditsan nodded, spoke in Navajo to his men inside, and all of them made way to their horses and the other half of their party. Nothing was said except between braves along the one hour trip back, and then a campfire was lit and food was eaten and they all sat around the fire to talk.

After Aditsan listened carefully to Luke who spoke for five minutes straight, his eyes grew wide, his mouth sneered, and he translated the ugly news. Some reacted by standing up, yelling, kicking the dirt, raising their hands in protest. Their leader sat still and silent. Luke didn't move, then when it was quiet, he spoke.

"My friend, shall I tell you we can fight this? Can I say good things? Or should I, should I tell you there are enough of these Apache to wipe us out right now. They will not accept our will. And my friend, there are more . . . there are many, many more White Men coming, too many for you to count. They will have their way. They will bring guns that will mow you and your family down in a moment. They will not care. They will not listen. They will not talk. They will just kill. I know that, now, and Slaughter is only one now, but later there will be many men like him."

Luke abruptly stood and had to walk away from the men, away from the heat of the fire, into the dark. He felt his body shake, and had an urgent desire to hurt that man who told him those things tonight. And he'd never felt so helpless in his life.

He sat beside Charlotte, and he cried. He ducked his head almost in shame as a part of this movement of white wolves devouring red men. He was exhausted and lay on the ground and slept.

Aditsan c. 1880

The sun woke him, and he stood to stretch and pat down his horse. He looked up to see his friend by the remains of last night's fire, staring into the embers. Luke walked over to him and sat next to him. He sighed.

"The Lieutenant, *that* White Man, he will not listen. Me, *this* White Man, I am now–your enemy." Luke choked at the realization that as a White Man, by association, was *the enemy.*

Aditsan rose and urged Luke to walk with him away from the camp, up atop a low hill. They both faced the coming sunrise in a cloudless sky. It was the beginning of summer and already warm. There was only a slight breeze. Noon would come in four hours. Noon meant death one of two ways. Slowly, or quickly, depending on the Chief's decision and commands to his people.

"You will go now, Luke, you will return home."

"No."

"This is my hell, not yours. You tried to speak for me and he would not hear."

"You can go into New Mexico for a time, and be safer than here. I can help."

"No. We will stay here. This is our home, safe or not."

"I will stay because I want to. It is not finished."

Aditsan was silent. Then he spoke the words of truth.

"It is finished."

Luke turned to face his friend and asked,

"What will you do today?"

"I will do what I must do for Navajo to live. But, I will not live their life."

Luke digested that slowly, and would, slowly, for the rest of his life.

He allowed Aditsan to take his hand, and pull him to his chest. When Luke saw his face grow wet with tears, he jerked his head down and cried. It was July second, 1890.

Arizona Territory c. 1890

It was July third, 1890. The United States of America was 104 years old in one day. The road was dusty and hot, and poor Charlotte had to bear the brunt of Luke's desire to be home with little rest, but she was up for it, as usual.

Luke didn't eat but some fry-bread since he left his best friend on that mound. He took water, and knew where to take his mount for her share. They rested for short lengths of time, but mostly galloped or loped his way south to his family he'd been away from for only days, but it felt like weeks, months, too much time.

He could see nature's signs of Lonesome Valley, and knew he was close. It was before sun up but they made it home on the fourth. Before taking care of Charlotte, he tied her up at the house and practically fell through the door. He just stood there, in the open hall, at the base of the stairs. It was dead silent, then he could hear Toby barking wildly, and then he saw her feet under a long nightgown and she fairly screamed when she gazed at him inside of their house.

It took two moments for them to hug each other, and Luke laughed and she cried and she started coffee while he washed himself off of all that he'd been through. He first took care of his mare and greeted Bandit and fed and watered them both and well. Charlotte was dirty and matted and exhausted but she was strong and glad to see her friend again.

The two sat at the table and Luke just let Tabitha talk and he listened.

"I missed you; we missed you so much! Renee and I have been inseparable since you left. We also worked a lot at the school. Also, here. I–just wanted to keep busy while you were gone."

Today, she'll be over with her wagon to take me, I mean us! It's the Main Event at the rodeo today, and there'll be fireworks too, but, only if you're wanting to."

Luke nodded, sat back, and just let himself smile listening to her enthusiasm, youth and joy of life her mother used to call, "joie de vivre", love of life. And his daughter was all that and more. It felt so wonderful to be there to witness it, especially as her father.

"I went by your office and your deputies were so kind! Ray took me to lunch and he is really interested in painting. He showed me some of his work, and I think he is quite talented. Mary at the Palace was asking when you'd be back, you know she thinks highly of you."

Luke raised his eyebrows.

"I see I'll need to talk to Ray tomorrow. . ."

Tabitha smiled silently at him, raising her eyebrows.

She got him more coffee, and toast with butter and jam, and then she noticed as she returned to the dining room to get the dishes that he had nodded off in his chair. At first, she was alarmed, thinking something was wrong with him. Then she just realized he was thoroughly tired to the bone and needed to sleep. Gently, she stirred him, and without a word or hesitation, she helped him up the stairs, took off his boots, and closed the door behind her.

Renee burst into the house and found Tabitha in the kitchen, packing their lunch in a basket and she moved to the fridge to get out cold lemonade before Tabitha could tell her who was home.

"He is probably deep asleep right now."

Renee folded her hands together and said,

"I'll just peek in!"

Renee stepped out of her shoes and walked barefoot down the hall, opening her love's bedroom door, then stepping on the carpet to pad over to his side. She tucked her feet underneath her and sat on the floor, staring into his face. His eyes were closed, he snored very quietly, his arms were across his chest. He was fully clothed without his boots and totally passed out. He was just sweet looking, innocent, she might even say beautiful to her.

And then something happened that had never happened in her 33 years of life. She knew, without a doubt, that this was a turning point in her life, in their lives. She didn't know how she knew, but she would marry this man, and spend the rest of her life with him. She felt like a girl and a woman all at once. She wanted to wake him, to tell him this wonderful news, but she couldn't. It was excruciatingly painful. But she remained there until her feet started to fall asleep, then she carefully and quietly left.

Instead, she and Tabitha took the wagon, their picnic lunch and lawn blankets to the Oldest Rodeo in America. She watched horses and bulls buck, ten-gallon hats fly through the air, and smelled the barbecues taking place around town and at the fair booths.

Tabitha held her parasol overhead to deflect the sun and walked with Renee, feeling unrelenting heat yet enjoying all the action going on around them. She noticed Ray in the crowd, towering above all others in the crowd. She caught his eye and instantly had the biggest, dumbest smile she'd ever seen. It made her laugh, and she tossed her head to the side and put a hand up to wave, but he was soon at her side and he walked with the two ladies for a few minutes.

Lunch was under a Cottonwood's shade on the grass for the three friends. The rodeo got underway and was very exciting. The musical bands played lively. But both ladies longed to be home with Luke, and got home before dusk to watch the fireworks.

Renee was unpacking the wagon and handing items to Tabitha. Renee started walking towards the door, and then saw Luke sitting in his chair. She set her things on the ground, and hurried to him as he stood to greet her.

He inhaled her freshness, remembering her scent of lemon and flowers.

He enveloped her in his arms.

"God, I missed you." He murmured into her left ear. He kissed that ear, and her neck, and then her mouth.

She didn't answer, she couldn't, she could only be held.

Tabitha took everything inside and stabled her horse, all while they had some time alone. As she walked up from the barn, the fireworks started, and suddenly the three of them were underneath an umbrella in the sky of colors and whistles and booms.

Luke and she embraced, emotionally grateful to be reunited. The three stood as the display of lights above made them ooh and aah. They then entered the house and shared a simple meal together. Renee opened a bottle of wine. Tabitha had a glass herself, and they toasted to Luke's safe return. But soon, Luke and Renee said their goodnights to her and Toby and headed upstairs to be alone.

Tabitha went out on the porch to enjoy the stars and think about the past few hours with a smile on her face and a sense of peace.

Upstairs, a man and a woman were making love in the dark, declaring their love for each other, and feeling completely connected with another human being for the first time ever.

In the morning, Luke told Renee all about his adventure, and though he shared the same story with Tab, he left out some of the ugliness for her sake. It could wait.

Renee and Luke Richmond c. 1890

Renee and Luke married that fall, "jumping the broom" at the new City Plaza lawn, inviting almost everyone in the town to attend. Renee was pregnant at the time, so they spent their honeymoon adding on to their ranch house and barn. Sheriff "Buckey O'Neill" had served as Sheriff of Prescott before Luke, and had kept the title even after Luke was sworn in. But in 1895, Luke decided to realize his dream and built and ran a small but highly-lauded horse ranch, his dream. "Bucky" ran again and served until he died.

They had three children over the next decade, and six grandchildren later in life. They were happy and traveled to Paris, France where Renee bought a new hat and several silk scarves in honor of her mother.

Luke told Tab the whole ugly story later on while she was attending college and became an advocate for women's rights. She became a Sociologist and taught at the University of Phoenix. She spent many weekends with Renee and Luke. She was often accompanied by her friend and colleague, Anabelle O'Neill, sister to Pauline who was a popular Suffragist living in San Francisco. Anabelle and Renee worked within the newly-formed Arizona Suffrage Association to legally allow taxpaying women the right to vote in school board elections. They were in meetings with Governor Wooley at the time, but learned that change took long and hard time. They each never married, yet were inseparable and lived out their years together in a home in Mesa. They both took a trip to Washington to meet President Harrison to discuss the many problems Native Americans were facing without seeing any change in their lifetimes.

Both his wife and his daughter had noticed a deeply centered change in Luke ever since he had returned from the north to help his Navajo friend. It was a shift in his very being of a kind. They accepted and loved him even more those early days after the tragedy he endured in losing his best friend. He was more serious and less excitable about things, less joyful, but so very loveable.

Sophia stayed married to Randolph in spite of his unfaithful behaviors, once and again in the future. He entered into politics and ran a close race for Governorship of New York. That is, while paying the price: he was locked into an abhorrent expensive legal contract drawn up by her father's lawyer, at Margaret's insistence, in perpetuity (ie., for the rest of his life). This was so that his secret affair was kept quiet.

He also had to sign over his largest of assets to his lovely wife, Sophia, which at her death would go immediately and completely to her daughter, Tabitha. This bribery strategy to keep his social and professional status pristine was why he drank himself to death just after the turn of the century.

Tabitha's later donation of much of this money to Arizona's public school system were very much appreciated and helpful in upgrading teaching and school hiring, buildings and supplies. Richmond Elementary School Library still stands in northern Phoenix, though it has since been closed and the building still stands vacant.

By the new millennium, 1900, most if not all of the Apache and Navajo people, as well as other trial natives were living on well-organized areas and tribal-named reservations on Arizona and New Mexico Territory land, as well as other states across the country. Aditsan was never accounted for on any rosters.

One morning during breakfast, Luke came across an article in the Arizona Republic about a Fort Apache incident where there was a revolt and the calvary were called. Unfortunately, Lt. Albert Slaughter and six other uniformed White Men working with him were overtaken and injured fatally. Something inside Luke unknotted, right at that moment, and he felt a letting go of a burning and festering resentment deep inside of him. He put down the paper, walked over to Renee, and held her from behind standing in the kitchen. He quietly told her who was now a dead man. She closed her eyes and sighed. They stood that way for several moments.

Epilogue c. 2022

It wasn't only the west that suffered; there were uprisings in the Midwest area of the country of note, as in Sitting Bull, the well-known Lakota Sioux medicine man. The Bull would die at the end of this era in history, but because of his own people taking the role of US Military Scouts. Meaning, they were paid soldiers to fight against desperate tribes who worked against the immigration of the new settlers. Hundreds of Natives were killed for the "big plan" to boundary the Natives and take over the vast land with rich resources that lay before the easterners now turned westerners.

The political philosophy was to take over the land, and if the Natives stand in the way, eliminate them, and for those who do not protest, pretend to take care of them on boundary reservation.

The problem with this simplified plan was that the Apache were the raiders that caused the settlers to feel threatened enough that the government felt their best neutral zone was a reservation. The Navajo, however, were not aggressive marauders, and therefore, should be deemed worthy of the land they already inhabited and had settled in for decades prior to the settler's arrival. There was a sense of "ownership" already in place. Why must they tolerate their land being shrunk to the NE acreage and overlapping into New Mexico.

President Harrison in 1890 had put immeasurable and valuable resources into the westward expansion into the acquisition of land and resources to become part of the country's holdings. The desire to use the land, the natural resources, and the available manpower of the indigenous population to further enrich those in power became too attractive an opportunity to halt due to ethical reasons.

When armies with rifles, men and women with societal dictates, having lived in abodes and cities that were highly evolved, including the rites of marriage, morals, laws, rules and common understanding came upon these Native women and men wearing animal skins living in animal skins tents, with their stone hammers and bows to be shot from arrows, tomahawks and knives as their only weapons, and no concept of anything except survival, there must have been a moment of surprise, acknowledgement, and then action which impacted those peoples very lives.

This was their way of saying, "You are beneath and behind us by centuries. Let us take control of your world to teach you how to live a better life, and we will keep the land." Land to the White Man was different than it was in England. There was so much, at least eight times as much as the whole of Great Britain.

"Hankering" was the "mot nouveau" for this era of history; a time for reimagining, and that was at first the beautiful part of the New World pioneering at this time in history. It was a chance to restructure the lives of those who were poor, or new immigrants, or prior slaves post-Civil War. There were regions that offered everything for the explorer; high, cold elevations in Montana and Colorado teeming with wild game, hot, dry deserts in California,

Arizona, and New Mexico that held acres of land and veins of ore containing gold and silver for the ambitious miner.

The flat prairies for farming like Kansas, Arkansas, Nebraska, Ohio, and Iowa offered acres and acres of loam for planting on farms and ranches.

It would seem to be enough for both Natives and newcomers, and perhaps it started out as a way to teach and guide the primitive to the more sophisticated ways of life. But the matter of force and control took over as the stronger desire.

Tomes have been written about wars and their horrors. Unfortunately, there are quiet wars that are accepted and are given life over many decades. There have been world leaders that have justified the evils of greed, racism, and ignoring the various mental illnesses that befall the human being, no matter race, color or creed.

There are 500,000 American Bison left from the 35,000,000 once roaming the plains since a count was first made. "We recognize the bison as a symbol of **strength and unity**," according to Fred DuBray, a member of the Cheyenne River Sioux Community (no longer referring to themselves as belonging to a "tribe") and once President of the ITBC. (Inter-Tribal Bison Cooperative) Sadly, the irresponsible populations who moved in to replace all indigenous communities and come away with any resources of value missed the point of those two descriptions of the noble bovine beast. The very survival of millions depended on the bison population flourishing; the many ways of utilizing almost every single part of the animal for their survival (meat, bone, hide, rawhide, horns, hair (wool), fat, teeth, hooves, tail, muscle, sinew). Spiritually, the bison was used in many ceremonies imperative to their daily lives. Imagine the horror of hungry scouts looking for food for their starving community and happening upon hundreds of Bison carcasses lying useless in waste under the harsh sun of the plains, spoiling for nothing but one bullseye hit successfully . . .

Impacts of such irresponsible actions are still happening today. As history has shown us, many are irreparable. No other animal has been lauded as so important to human survival and progression over many centuries of time. To look into the eyes this living breathing creature also has an impact. Actually nearsighted, they have a heightened sense of smell. Their color ranges from amber to brown-black. They rarely blink. You get the feeling you are staring into an "old soul" of a kind. Just their presence renders a feeling of majesty, power, size and history. You wonder if she, or he feels sadness that so many of their ancestors have suffered such loss of their own, perhaps, as a type of genocide.

Author's Note

I am grateful for a renewed knowledge of American history during this time. I have tried to use authentic language of the era. I am planning a visit to Arizona's Navajo Nation after acquisition of a permit to hopefully learn more. I have lived in Prescott Valley for almost five years and plan to remain. I hope to view a herd of Bison roaming relatively free . . . someday soon. Thank you for reading my tale. I plan to write a sequel entitled, ***The Coyote.***

Author Bio

Karen Keim has been writing stories since she was 13 years old, following her father's spare-time nightly and weekend compulsion. She taught the second grade for many years after getting her BA degree at UCSB in California. Working long-term on a memoir, she loves telling stories with historical settings, and always includes a romance within a social issue. Karen is married and lives in Prescott, Arizona. She practices yoga, tutors privately and enjoys hiking with her husband, Harry. Rubie, her Chihuahua-mix and her two Siamese (sisters) are all adopted and very much a major part of their family.

Author Bio

Karen Keim has been writing stories since she was 13 years old, following her father's spare-time nightly and weekend compulsion. She taught the second grade for many years after getting her BA degree at UCSB in California. Working long-term on a memoir, she loves telling stories with historical settings, and always includes a romance within a social issue. Karen is married and lives in Prescott, Arizona. She practices yoga, tutors privately and enjoys hiking with her husband, Harry. Rubie, her Chihuahua-mix and her two Siamese (sisters) are all adopted and very much a major part of their family.

~   ~

CPSIA information can be obtained
at www.ICGtesting.com
Printed in the USA
JSHW012035070723
44199JS00001B/3